AAHANA

A STRANGER WHO BROUGHT SUNSHINE

VASANTH PEMMADI

With the blessings of my late father,

Sri. Pemmadi Murali Krishna Garu (1976-2024)

Contents

Contents

I dedicate this book to all the ladies who are my sunshine in
life:

My mother, Pemmadi Baby Rani,
My sister, Tirumalasetti Sruthi,
and all the next generation kids in my family:
My daughters,
Karri Heshvika Aadhya,
Karri Diviksha Sri Vasuki,
Balasadi Diyaanshi.

Preface

My name is Vasanth Pemmadi. While you may have already read my author bio, I'd like to share a bit more about myself. I am a passionate writer, but more importantly, I am a passionate storyteller. I love narrating stories, and whether the medium changes, the essence remains the same.

"Aahana" holds a special place in my heart. During my B.Tech days around 2017-18, I began writing many stories in my mother tongue, but I never seen them through to the end. Then came "Aahana," my first ever completed story, which I am incredibly proud of. Initially, I thought of approaching some film industry individuals to bring "Aahana" to the screen, but life took unexpected turns, and I lost track, leaving me alone.

Years passed, and "Aahana" remained just a folder in my system, untouched and unread. Then, in 2024, my best friend and I started our very own movie review blogspot, **Vasi and Phani Reviews**. This venture sparked a change in my life. After successfully reviewing several movies, I felt a strong urge to make "Aahana" public. Even if it reached only a few people, I wanted to share it with the world.

With that thought in mind, I began transforming "Aahana" into a book. The journey wasn't easy; I faced numerous challenges. However, those challenges led me to this moment, where you are holding my story in your hands. I hope "Aahana" resonates with you and touches your heart just as it has touched mine.

Thank you for being part of this journey.

— Vasanth Pemmadi

Acknowledgements

The book version of "Aahana" began with the initial push from our review blogspot, **Vasi and Phani Reviews**, which was founded by me and my best friend, **Kalidindi Sivaphaneendra**. Sivaphaneendra, or Phani as I fondly call him, has been more than a friend throughout this journey—he has been my anchor, my support system, and my biggest cheerleader.

Phani was the first listener of "Aahana" and later, the first reader of its book version. From the moment the idea took root, he stood by me, offering unwavering support and encouragement. I often joke about how I irritated him to the extent that he started dreaming about "Aahana," but in truth, his patience and persistence were invaluable. From the beginning to the end, Phani was there, helping me navigate the complexities of storytelling and refining my unconventional scenes by always asking, "how" and "why."

Our friendship dates back to our college days, and even then, Phani was my sounding board. I must have asked him a thousand times how we could bring "Aahana" to life. Whenever I called him during those years when "Aahana" was just a folder on my system, he would smile and listen, never once dismissing my dreams. When I finally decided to turn "Aahana" into a book, Phani gave his utmost support, helping me make this dream a reality.

A special mention goes to all my family members who never laughed at my ambition to write a book. Their belief in me—that I could achieve anything I set my mind to—was a source of immense strength. Their faith often surpassed my own confidence, providing the encouragement I needed to keep pushing forward.

To Phani, for being there from the inception of "Aahana" to its completion, and to my family, for their unwavering belief and support—thank you. This journey would not have been possible without you.

— Vasanth Pemmadi

"*What made "Aahana" possible for me was embracing the journey one step at a time. When I started writing this book, I never thought about the ending. I only focused on the next step, moving forward incrementally. Just like that, one step forward, step by step.*
Remember, never think too far into the future. Do things at your own pace, step by step."

— Vasanth Pemmadi

Prologue

Rajeev Gandhi International Airport buzzes with activity. The air is filled with the sounds of announcements, the hum of conversations, and the rolling of luggage wheels. The scent of freshly brewed coffee from nearby cafes mingles with the faint aroma of airport cleaning products. Travelers move with purpose, some in a hurry to catch their flights, others leisurely waiting for their departure time.

In the midst of this busy scene, a quiet corner of the airport lounge offers a haven of calm. Comfortable chairs are arranged neatly, and a large window provides a view of the airplanes taking off and landing. The soft lighting and the gentle murmur of the lounge create a peaceful atmosphere.

Sitting in one of these chairs is a man, his posture relaxed yet alert. His name is Surya. He glances around the lounge, taking in the diverse crowd of travelers before turning his attention to the notebook on his lap. He looks up, catching your gaze, and a warm smile spreads across his face.

"My name is Surya," he begins, his voice steady and inviting. "Today, I am going to narrate my story to you."

Surya's eyes reflect a depth of experience and emotion as he prepares to share his journey. His story, like the bustling airport around him, is filled with moments of departure and arrival, of joy and sorrow. As he begins to speak, the world outside the lounge fades away, and you are drawn into the captivating tale of Aahana.

CHAPTER I

The Beginning

It's a rainy day, and the atmosphere in our house is as stormy as the weather outside. The relentless downpour creates a continuous symphony of raindrops against the window panes, a stark contrast to the silence that occasionally settles after each thunderous argument between my parents.

My name is Surya, and I am six years old this year. This is the house where I live. The house is modest, with peeling wallpaper and creaky wooden floors that groan under every step. The furniture is worn, the fabric of the couch threadbare from years of use. The dim lighting in the kitchen does little to hide the signs of neglect and wear. The single bulb casts an eerie glow, creating a stark contrast between light and shadow that mirrors the turmoil in our lives. The windows are streaked with rain, blurring the view of the world outside, as if the house itself is crying.

The dark clouds above mirror the gloom that pervades our home, casting long shadows that dance ominously on the walls of our small, cluttered house.

Every day in this house, there are quarrels. My father, with his bloodshot eyes and the stench of alcohol on his breath, is addicted to drinking. His addiction transforms him from the loving father I barely remember into a volatile presence, always on the brink of an outburst. Because of this, he always fights with my mother.

My mother was once a vibrant woman with dreams of her own. She wanted to be a teacher, to inspire young minds and make a difference in the world. But life had other plans. She fell in love with my father, and their love story, once so full of promise, now feels like a distant memory. The weight of broken dreams and constant fights has taken a toll on her, turning her into a shadow of the woman she once was.

My mother, who once had a bright smile and a contagious laugh, now wears a constant expression of sorrow and fatigue. These fights are loud and scary, making the walls of our small home tremble with anger and fear. The rain patters incessantly against the window panes, a soundtrack to the chaos within, each drop echoing the tears I've seen my mother shed countless times.

Tonight, my uncle comes over to try to resolve the issue again. His presence is a rare beacon of calm in our turbulent household. My uncle is a tall, kind man with gentle eyes that always seem to carry a hint of sadness. He tries his best to mediate between my parents, but his efforts often feel like trying to stop a storm with a whisper. I can hear the shouting from my room, where I hide under the covers, wishing it would all go away. The voices of my parents rise and fall like the crashing waves of a stormy sea, punctuated by the occasional sob from my mother.

"Surya, come here," my uncle calls out gently, finding me huddled on my bed. His voice is a soothing balm amidst the uproar. He lifts me up and takes me to the kitchen, where my mother sits, her face streaked with tears. The kitchen is dimly lit, the single bulb casting long shadows that seem to dance with the turmoil in our hearts. The flickering light highlights the deep lines of worry etched on my mother's face, making her look older than she is.

I look at my uncle, confused and frightened. His face is lined with worry, his eyes soft but sad. "Uncle, why do my parents always fight? Why did they get together if they can't even stand each other?" I ask, my young mind struggling to grasp the complexities of adult relationships.

He sighs deeply, a sound that seems to carry the weight of the world. He pulls me onto his lap, wrapping his arms around me protectively. "Surya, sometimes people make mistakes. Sometimes hearts don't align, even if they are together physically. Bringing two people together is easy, but uniting their hearts is very difficult. We forced two people to be together, even though their hearts couldn't unite," he explains, his voice tinged with regret and sadness.

I glance at my mother, her eyes red and puffy from crying. She looks at me with a mixture of love and pain, her hands trembling as she clutches a handkerchief. The room feels heavy with unspoken words and shattered dreams. The air is thick with a palpable tension, making it hard to breathe.

"But wouldn't they be happier if they weren't together?" I ask, still trying to understand. The idea of happiness seems so far removed from our daily reality.

"Why can't they take a divorce and move on?" I added, recalling the term I'd overheard from our neighbour.

"Who said that word 'divorce' to you, Surya?" my uncle asks, surprised by my use of such a grown-up term.

"Uncle, the neighbour next door. Whenever there is a fight, he always says that," I reply, looking at him for answers.

My uncle's face softens further, a flicker of sorrow crossing his features. "Divorce isn't as simple as you think. It's not just a solution to stop fighting; it changes everything, including your life. Divorce means breaking the promise of responsibility towards each other, and it impacts everyone involved, including you," he explains gently, his voice a mix of patience and sorrow.

My uncle often reflects on his own life, the choices he made, and how they led him to this point. He thinks about his younger years, full of hope and dreams, and how life's hardships have shaped him into a man who carries the weight of his family's troubles on his shoulders. He remembers the time when my parents were in love, their laughter filling the house with joy. He wonders where it all went wrong, and if there was something he could have done to prevent this downfall.

As I listen, I try to understand the gravity of his words. My young mind struggles to comprehend the depth of the situation, but I can sense the pain it causes. The rain outside continues to fall, each drop a reminder of the tears shed within these walls.

My father's shouts pierce through the momentary silence, and I flinch, burying my face in my uncle's shoulder. My uncle strokes my hair, trying to comfort me. "Surya, sometimes we hold onto things because we believe it's for the best, even if it causes pain. Your parents are trying to do what they think is right, even if it doesn't seem that way."

I nod, though I'm not sure I fully understand. The concept of right and wrong blurs in the face of constant conflict. My mother's sobs quiet down, replaced by a heavy, oppressive silence. My father retreats to his room, slamming the door behind him. The house, once again, falls into an uneasy calm.

"Uncle, will it ever get better?" I ask, my voice barely above a whisper.

He looks at me, his eyes filled with a mixture of hope and sadness. "I don't know, Surya. But I promise you this: I will always be here for you, no matter what. You are not alone."

Those words, simple yet profound, give me a sliver of comfort. I cling to them, hoping that one day, the storm will pass, and peace will return to our home. For now, I take solace in my uncle's embrace, finding a momentary refuge from the chaos that surrounds us.

The rain continues its relentless downpour, but in my uncle's arms, I find a brief respite, a small island of safety amidst the turbulent sea of my young life. And as I drift into a restless sleep, I hold onto the hope that someday, things will change for the better. The flickering light casts shadows that seem to tell their own stories on the walls, stories of sorrow, hope, and the promise of a brighter future.

After few days. "Mom, why do you cry so much?" I ask one day, finding her alone in the kitchen, staring out the window at the rain.

She looks at me, her eyes filled with unshed tears. "Oh, Surya, sometimes life doesn't turn out the way we hope," she says, her voice trembling. "But that doesn't mean we stop hoping for better days."

"But can't we make it better?" I persist, my young heart aching to fix the brokenness I see around me.

She sighs, pulling me into a hug. "Some things are beyond our control, dear. But we can still find moments of happiness, even in the darkest times. And we must hold onto those moments, no matter how small they seem."

I can't understand the depth of my mother words but I know that I am the one she is finding her happiness in.

After those days passed, with the usual fights and cries in the house.

One rare sunny day, my uncle takes me to the park. It's a small escape from the constant fighting at home, a place where I can be a child without the weight of my family's troubles. We play on the swings, and for a moment, I forget about the chaos waiting for us at home. My uncle watches me with a smile, but I can see the worry in his eyes, even as he tries to hide it.

"Uncle, why can't every day be like this?" I ask, breathless from running around.

He ruffles my hair, his expression bittersweet. "Life has its ups and downs, Surya. But it's these moments of joy that give us the strength to get through the tough times. Remember this feeling, and hold onto it."

As we leave the park, I feel a sense of hope, a belief that there are still good things in the world, even if they seem few and far between. And I carry that hope with me, a small light in the darkness of my young life.

CHAPTER II

The Aftermath of Loss

One evening, things get worse than usual. The fights that night is louder, more vicious. My father's voice is a roar, my mother's a desperate plea. The crashing of dishes and the shattering of glass echo through the house, mingling with the relentless rain outside. My mother takes my hand, her grip tight and trembling, and leads me out of the house. The night is cold, and the rain soaks us to the bone, but the storm outside seems almost gentle compared to the turmoil within our home. We go to my uncle's home for refuge, seeking solace from the relentless conflict.

My mother, worn out from the constant fighting, confides in her brother. I hear them talking in hushed tones, their words a lifeline in the midst of our shared despair. The living room is dimly lit, the shadows long and dark, matching the mood. My mother sits on the old, worn couch, her face pale and tear-streaked. The weight of years of unhappiness has etched deep lines into her once-vibrant face.

"Brother, I can't do this anymore," she says, her voice breaking with each word. "I thought I could make it work, but every day is a struggle. I feel like I'm losing myself." Her eyes, once bright with hope, now reflect only exhaustion and sorrow.

My uncle listens patiently, offering his support. His hand rests gently on her shoulder, a silent promise of unwavering support. "You are strong, but you don't have to go through this alone. Surya and you can stay here as long as you need," he says softly. His voice is steady, a stark contrast to the chaos we've left behind.

I watch them, feeling a mixture of relief and confusion. My mother's pain is now more evident to me than ever before. The house is quiet, the only sound the ticking of the old grandfather clock, a reminder of the passage of time and the fragility of our existence.

As the days pass, I start living with my uncle. The adjustment to the new environment is slow, each day a battle against the lingering memories of my parents' fights. My uncle's home is warm and inviting, filled with the comforting smells of home-cooked meals and the gentle hum of daily life. But questions linger in my mind, gnawing at me like a persistent itch. One day, I gather the courage to ask my uncle.

"Uncle, why do people get married if they can't get along? Why do they stay together and fight?" I ask, my voice small and uncertain. The weight of my question hangs in the air, heavy and unanswerable.

He looks at me thoughtfully before answering, his eyes searching for the right words. "Surya, relationships are complicated. Sometimes people hope things will get better, or they stay together for the sake of their children. But it's not always the right choice," he says, his tone gentle yet firm.

"Divorce is not just a word. It's a change, a big change. It means they give up their responsibilities towards each other, and that affects everyone, especially children," he explains, his voice tinged with a sadness that I don't fully understand.

"But wouldn't I be happier if they were apart?" I ask, still trying to make sense of it all. The idea of happiness seems distant and elusive.

"It's not that simple. Life after divorce can be difficult too, with its own set of challenges," he says, patting my head gently. His words offer a glimpse into the complexities of adult life, a world that seems both confusing and daunting.

• • •

Years passed, and the constant turmoil within our home took a severe toll on my father. His addiction to alcohol grew worse, consuming him from the inside out. The once-strong man I knew became a shadow of himself, his eyes hollow and distant. One fateful night, he drank far more than his fragile body could handle. I remember the moment vividly—his face pale and lifeless, the empty bottle lying beside him like a cruel mockery of his lost battle. The house fell into a haunting silence that was almost deafening. Despite all the chaos and resentment, I harboured, the sight of my father's lifeless body filled me with a profound sorrow. He was gone, and with him, a part of my turbulent childhood ended.

The days that followed were a blur of grief and confusion. My mother, who had endured years of pain and suffering, was left utterly devastated by my father's death. She wept uncontrollably, her cries echoing through the empty halls of our home. The strength she had shown throughout the years seemed to vanish, leaving behind a fragile shell of the woman she once was. Despite my efforts to console her, she grew weaker each day, consumed by her sorrow. It wasn't long before she too succumbed to the weight of her grief, her heart unable to bear the loss. One morning, I found her lifeless beside my father's photograph, her tears dried on her cheeks. In losing her, I felt a part of my soul being ripped away.

With both my parents gone, I found myself thrust into a world of solitude. My uncle took me in, offering me a place in his home, but nothing could fill the void left by their absence. I became a loner, retreating further into myself with each passing day. Social interactions felt meaningless, and the world around me seemed distant and uninviting. My cousin Swecha tried to reach out, her attempts at friendship sincere, but my heart was too guarded, too broken to respond. I moved through life like a ghost, haunted by memories of a family torn apart and the deep-seated fears that had taken root in my heart. The once-vivid colours of my childhood had faded into a dull, unending grey.

Each day felt like an endless cycle of sorrow and numbness. The laughter and joy that once filled our home were replaced by a haunting silence. I spent hours staring out of the window, watching the world move on without me. School became a place of escape, where I could lose myself in books and lessons, but even there, the shadow of my past lingered.

My uncle, though kind and caring, struggled to reach me. He tried to fill the void left by my parents, but the wounds were too deep. I could see the worry in his eyes, the helplessness of watching a child retreat into a shell of pain. He spoke to me often, sharing stories of my parents from happier times, trying to spark a connection. But my heart was closed off, a fortress built to protect against further hurt.

One evening, as we sat by the fireplace, my uncle shared a story from his childhood. "Surya, your father and I used to play cricket in the fields behind our house. He was always the best batsman, and I was the one chasing the ball. Those were simpler times, filled with laughter and dreams," he said, his eyes distant as he recalled the past.

I listened, my heart aching with a mixture of longing and resentment. I missed the father I barely knew, the mother who had been my rock. Their absence was a constant reminder of the fragility of life, of the pain that lurked in every corner.

Despite my uncle's efforts, the darkness within me grew. I avoided my friends, preferring the solitude of my room. The walls became my companions, the silence my refuge. The days turned into weeks, and the weeks into months, each one blending into the next in a monotonous blur.

One day, as I sat in my room, my cousin Swecha (My uncle's daughter) knocked on the door. "Surya, can I come in?" she asked, her voice gentle and cautious. I nodded, not trusting myself to speak.

She entered, carrying a small box. "I found something that might cheer you up," she said, opening the box to reveal old photographs of our parents. "Look, here they are at a family picnic. And this one, at a festival," she said, showing me each picture. I can already grasp the situation she is eagerly trying to lighten my mood.

As I looked at the photographs, memories flooded back. I saw my parents' smiles, their happiness captured in those fleeting moments. I can feel my emotions deep inside starting crumbling. Swecha hugged me, her warmth a balm to my wounded soul.

But all her empathy and care towards me, I can feel it, but I have no reason to respond or reciprocate the same feeling towards her. I have faced so much in this small life of mine to even reconsider any feelings targeted towards me.

I want only solitude right now because I find solace in that and nothing else.

$$***$$

The days after passed in a blurr

After that, days passed like seasons. My cousin Swecha tries her best to appeal to me, that she is someone who is going to stay by my side. Despite the continuous attempts of my cousin Swecha to break through my walls, she eventually understood that I needed my own time to move on from the traumatic experiences of my past. The days passed by in a blur, and the healing process was slow and arduous. I completed my schooling and my +1 and +2 in my hometown, Bhimavaram. Then, my uncle had to relocate for his job, and I followed him to Hyderabad. There, I completed my B. Tech with good grades, which eventually led to a job offer from TCS.

Throughout these years, nothing particularly special happened in my life. The people I met quickly realized the kind of person I was—a moody individual who preferred solitude. They noticed my reluctance to form close relationships, and most weren't inclined to try. This suited me perfectly. I avoided friendships and didn't form ties beyond what was absolutely necessary. I never exchanged phone numbers without a proper reason. Even during my B. Tech days, I maintained minimal contact with my project teammates, ensuring that my detachment did not put the team in any difficult situations. I led my life in such a way that I remained insulated from potential hurt.

I had effectively put myself in a bubble, a protective shield against the world. In TCS, I opted for the night shift from the start, planning to meet as few people as possible. I wasn't a crowd person, so the night shift seemed like the perfect solution. Thus began my autopilot life—a life devoid of significant human interaction or emotional entanglement.

CHAPTER III

A Life on Autopilot

Every day, my life begins at dusk. The alarm clock buzzes sharply at 6 PM, its sound cutting through the heavy silence of my room. The jarring noise drags me from the clutches of sleep, a reluctant return to consciousness. I deliberately chose the night shift at TCS to avoid the bustling daytime world, finding solace in the quiet of the night. The darkness outside feels like a protective shroud, concealing me from the brightness that once promised hope and now feels overwhelming.

My mornings are everyone else's evenings, and as I groggily rise from my bed, the city outside my window transitions from daylight to twilight. I move through my small room at my uncle's house with mechanical precision—brushing my teeth, taking a quick shower, and dressing in the same rotation of clothes. The routine is unchanging, offering a strange comfort in its predictability.

The walls of my room are a dull grey, adorned with a few photographs of my parents, their faces frozen in happier times. The small details of my day are what tether me to reality. Each night, as I prepare for work, I take a moment to gaze at the photographs on my wall. My mother's smile, radiant and full of life, is a stark contrast to the hollow eyes that haunt my dreams. My father, once a pillar of strength, now a distant memory, reminds me of the fragility of happiness. These images, both a comfort and a torment, are all I have left of a past that feels more like a dream than a reality.

As I step out of my room, I often find Swecha, my cousin, waiting for me with a warm smile and hopeful eyes.

I always come out in a hurry so that I can grab my meal in the earliest, Swecha's attempts to connect with me are a constant in my life. Her perseverance is almost admirable, though I wish she would understand that some wounds take more than kind words to heal.

She tries to engage me in conversation, her efforts to draw me out both touching and painful. Despite my reluctance, I appreciate her persistence, even if I can't fully reciprocate her warmth.

"Surya, how was your day?" she asks, her voice filled with genuine curiosity.

"It was fine, Swecha. Just the usual," I reply, my voice devoid of enthusiasm. She looks at me, her eyes searching for any sign of emotion, but I offer none.

"Are you sure you don't want to join us for dinner tonight? Dad made your favourite dish," she adds, her tone hopeful.

"Thanks, but I'll pass. I'm not that hungry," I say, forcing a small smile to ease her disappointment.

After a brief and often one-sided exchange, I quietly leave for my office. My office is nearby the house so I take walk instead of my bike everyday so that my body would stay fit

My walks to and from the office are the only times I feel a semblance of peace. The quiet streets, the cool night air, and the distant hum of the city provide a backdrop for my thoughts. It's during these solitary moments that I allow myself to reflect on my life, to question the choices I've made and the person I've become.

The walk to the office is familiar, each step a part of the routine I have come to rely on. The streets are less crowded, the usual hustle and bustle of the city giving way to a quieter, more subdued atmosphere. The air is cooler, the sounds softer, and I find a strange solace in this nocturnal world.

My workday begins when most people are winding down theirs. I walk to the office, my steps steady but devoid of any eagerness. At TCS, my presence is barely acknowledged by my colleagues, who have come to accept my withdrawn demeanour. I sit at my desk, immersing myself in my tasks with a focus that borders on obsession. It's easier to lose myself in code and data than to confront the emptiness of my personal life.

The office is a maze of cubicles and computer screens, the dim glow of monitors casting an eerie light. My workstation is neatly organized, a stark contrast to the chaos in my mind.

At TCS, my work is my refuge. The complex algorithms and endless lines of code demand my full attention, leaving no room for the intrusive thoughts that plague me. My colleagues, accustomed to my silence, no longer attempt to draw me out of my shell. They see me as efficient and reliable, if a bit aloof, and for the most part, they leave me to my work.

My interactions with others are minimal, confined to polite nods and terse greetings. Phani, my only friend, breaks the monotony with a daily "hi" and "bye," his attempts at conversation falling into a predictable pattern.

Phani's attempts at friendship are a welcome distraction, though I can't bring myself to fully engage.

"Hey Surya, how's it going?" Phani asks, his voice a mix of concern and casual cheerfulness.

"Same as always, Phani. Just getting through the day," I reply, my tone flat.

"You should join us for a coffee break sometime. It might do you some good to get out of the office for a bit," he suggests, his smile warm and inviting.

"Maybe someday. Thanks for the offer," I say, knowing that someday might never come.

The hours pass in a blur of keystrokes and muted conversations, my mind locked in the safety of routine. The hum of the air conditioning, the clicking of keyboards, and the occasional murmur of conversation create a background noise that I have grown accustomed to. The predictability of it all is both comforting and suffocating.

When my shift ends, the world outside is shrouded in darkness. I leave the office as quietly as I arrived, avoiding any unnecessary interactions. The walk back home is a solitary journey, the streets mostly deserted at this late hour. The night air is cool, a gentle breeze rustling the leaves of the trees that line the sidewalk. The city lights cast long shadows, creating a landscape of light and dark that mirrors my inner turmoil.

I return to my room, the weight of the day's isolation settling heavily on my shoulders. I unwind by reading or staring blankly at the ceiling, my mind a swirl of unspoken thoughts and buried emotions. Books are my escape, the stories offering a temporary respite from my own reality. The characters' lives, filled with adventure and passion, contrast sharply with my own monotonous existence.

The nights blend into one another, each one a repetition of the last. My life, confined to the boundaries of routine, feels safe yet stifling. The books I read, the stories I lose myself in, provide a temporary escape from the monotony. Each character's journey, filled with trials and triumphs, contrasts sharply with my own stagnant existence.

As I lie in bed, I start flooding with thoughts for some time which make me uncomfortable sleeping but as time passes Sleep finally takes me, offering a brief respite before the cycle begins anew.

My life on autopilot, while predictable and safe, is also a prison of my own making. The walls I've built to protect myself from further pain have become barriers to any potential happiness. Yet, for now, it is the only way I know how to survive.

CHAPTER IV

Meeting a Stranger

Then came the day when everything seemed to go wrong. It started with waking up earlier than necessary, a rare and regrettable occurrence. Despite working the night shift, I found myself awake before dawn, unable to fall back to sleep. The alarm hadn't gone off yet, and the soft light of dawn crept through the curtains, casting a gentle glow in my room.

The room was bathed in a soft, almost ethereal light that painted everything in shades of pastel. It was the kind of light that usually brought a sense of peace, but today it felt like an unwelcome intruder. I lay in bed, my mind refusing to quiet down, thoughts bouncing around with nowhere to go. The silence of the early morning was both soothing and suffocating, a stark contrast to the usual calmer of my night shifts.

Aimlessly glued to my phone, I wasted time on social media and trivial games, trying to stave off the inevitable march towards another monotonous night at work. I scrolled through endless feeds of smiling faces, vacation photos, and inspirational quotes that felt hollow in the quiet of my room. Each swipe and tap seemed to echo in the stillness, a reminder of the empty hours stretching ahead.

My thumb moved mechanically, liking posts I barely glanced at, playing games that required no real thought. I watched short, looping videos that promised a momentary distraction but left me feeling more disconnected than before. The digital world, usually a reliable escape, felt particularly hollow this morning. It was as if the artificial glow of the screen couldn't compete with the natural dawn light filtering in, making my usual distractions seem even more futile.

Minutes turned into an hour, and I could feel the weight of the upcoming day pressing down on me. I glanced at the clock, hoping time had moved faster, but it hadn't. It was still too early to get ready for work, yet too late to try and get more sleep. I felt stuck in a liminal space, caught between the urge to be productive and the desire to just lay there, hoping for some kind of reprieve.

Eventually, I dragged myself out of bed, the sense of regret already settling in. I knew it was going to be one of those days where everything felt off, where each small inconvenience would feel like a personal affront. As I moved through the motions of getting ready, the early start weighed on me, a reminder that sometimes, even the simplest things can set the tone for a day when everything seems to go wrong.

After what felt like hours, I glanced at the time and realized it was still a bit early to head to the office. Despite this, I decided to get up and start my day. I freshened up, got ready, and found myself outside much earlier than my regular timing. Just as I stepped out, I saw Swecha returning from her shift.

"You're early today, Surya," she remarked, looking at her watch. "Is there a meeting or something?"

"No, I woke up early, that's all," I replied, offering a faint smile.

I headed to the office, trying to shake off the odd feeling that had settled over me. The office routine unfolded as usual—nothing special, just the same mundane tasks that filled my days with a numbing predictability. The hum of computers and the muted conversations of my colleagues created a monotonous symphony that usually blended into the background of my thoughts. The artificial light of the office felt harsh against the dim backdrop of my inner world, casting a sterile glow over everything.

As I settled into my desk, I began to feel a small semblance of comfort. My chair, though old, had always been my little corner of stability in the otherwise chaotic environment. I leaned back, trying to lose myself in the familiarity of the routine, when suddenly, a loud crank sound shattered the stillness. The noise was jarring, a sharp contrast to the usual subdued office sounds.

Before I could fully comprehend what was happening, the chair beneath me gave way with a violent snap. I felt a sickening lurch as I lost my balance and plummeted to the floor. The fall was abrupt and disorienting, the kind of unexpected jolt that leaves you momentarily breathless. I landed awkwardly, my body twisting in a futile attempt to break the fall. A sharp pain shot through my wrist as it took the brunt of the impact, and I knew immediately that something was wrong.

The humiliation of the moment hit me almost as hard as the physical pain. My face flushed with embarrassment, and a rush of heat surged to my cheeks. I could feel the eyes of my colleagues on me, their concerned faces blurring into a collective gaze of curiosity and pity. My heart raced, not just from the pain but from the anxiety of being the centre of attention in such an undignified manner.

As I lay there, stunned and trying to catch my breath, the sharp pain in my wrist intensified. It felt as though needles were being driven into my bones, and I cradled my injured hand close to my chest. The physical discomfort was matched only by the overwhelming desire to disappear, to melt away from the prying eyes and the whispered questions that filled the room.

The noise attracted a crowd of colleagues, their concerned faces converging around me like an unwanted spotlight. As someone who has always preferred the shadows, the sudden attention felt suffocating. My heart raced, not just from the pain in my hand but from the anxiety of being surrounded by so many people. Each concerned glance and intrusive question amplified my discomfort.

"Surya, are you okay?" one of them asked, their voice tinged with genuine concern.

"I... I'm fine," I stammered, my voice barely above a whisper. Desperate for some air and solitude, I waved them off. "I just need to breathe."

The words felt inadequate, but I couldn't muster more. I hurried outside, seeking refuge in the quiet corridors of the building, away from the prying eyes and overwhelming concern. The solitude was a welcome relief, allowing me to regain my composure and the sense of control that often eludes me in social situations.

With the pain in my hand growing, I decided to visit the hospital, fearing there might be a fracture. After assuring everyone that I was fine, I booked a Rapido and waited for the ride to arrive in front of the office. When the ride came and called, I went off to the ortho doctor nearby. The doctor's office was a sterile, impersonal place, the kind that makes you feel both insignificant and overly exposed. The doctor examined me, prescribed the necessary medication, and wrapped my hand in a bandage. Reassured that I was going to be fine, I stepped out of the examination room and took a seat in the lobby, waiting for my file to be processed.

As I sat there, dreading the inevitable barrage of questions from my colleagues about my injury, I tried to relax. It was one of the rare moments I could be alone with my thoughts, away from the prying eyes and constant chatter. The hospital lobby was a bustling place, filled with a mix of people. The hum of conversations, the occasional beep of medical equipment, and the soft footfalls of nurses created a background symphony of life. I sat in a corner, observing the flow of people and the stories they carried. It was a place of both hope and despair, where lives intertwined briefly before diverging again.

While waiting for my file in the hospital lobby, I tried to relax, pushing away thoughts of the inevitable barrage of questions from my colleagues about my injury. Then, something caught my eye—a file lying on a seat in the next row. At first, I dismissed it as none of my business, the introvert in me preferring to avoid any unnecessary interaction or attention. But then, I noticed something familiar about the ID card sticking out of it. It was the same TCS ID card.

My curiosity was piqued, a feeling unfamiliar and uncomfortable. For someone who usually kept to himself and avoided the spotlight, this sudden urge to investigate was entirely out of character. I glanced around nervously, ensuring no one was watching. My heart pounded, not just from the residual pain in my hand but from the anxiety of stepping out of my comfort zone. The idea of doing something so bold, so out of my ordinary routine, filled me with a mix of excitement and dread.

Seizing the moment, I moved quickly towards the file, each step feeling heavier with hesitation. Opening it cautiously, my hands slightly trembling, I saw the name "Aahana" on the cover and the ID card. My breath hitched as I continued reading, the word "Osteosarcoma" staring back at me from the medical report. I stood there, momentarily stunned, the name and the diagnosis echoing in my mind.

As I waited for my file in the hospital lobby, a surge of curiosity overtook me. I decided to look up the disease mentioned in the file. Pulling out my phone, I opened Google and typed "Osteosarcoma." To double-check the spelling, I reopened the file. Just as I was engrossed in the details, a girl appeared and stood next to me, her presence suddenly looming over my solitude.

The curiosity that led me to the file now filled me with a strange mix of concern and intrigue about Aahana, a person I had yet to meet but whose story was now inexplicably tied to my own. This was the first time in years that I had allowed myself to be drawn into someone else's life, driven by something other than necessity or obligation. It was as if the universe had thrown a lifeline into my monotonous existence, pulling me towards a story that was not my own but one that I couldn't ignore.

The hospital around me seemed to blur, my focus entirely on the file in my hands. My introverted nature made this small act of curiosity feel monumental. The idea of involving myself in someone else's life, even in such a minimal way, was daunting. For years, I had built walls around myself, keeping others at a distance to avoid the pain of loss and the discomfort of social interaction. Yet, here I was, standing in a hospital lobby, holding a stranger's file.

As I stood there, lost in thought, I felt a presence beside me.

"What are you doing with my file?" she asked, her voice tinged with a mix of irritation and curiosity.

CHAPTER V

Aahana

Startled, I quickly stood up and moved away, caught off guard by her sudden appearance. She was petite, with a frail yet determined air about her. Her eyes, though weary, held a spark of curiosity and resolve. Her presence commanded attention despite her delicate frame, and for a moment, I felt an inexplicable urge to apologize even before she spoke.

"Hey! What are you doing with my file?" she demanded, her voice firm and unyielding. The question hung in the air, filled with an intensity that made me hesitate.

I fumbled for words, caught in the act and feeling the weight of her gaze. After a moment of hesitation, I finally turned back, gathering the courage to face her.

There she stood, a young woman in her twenties with an ethereal beauty, like someone straight out of a fairy tale. Her face, though angry, exuded a calming presence. Even in her anger, she seemed serene, a contradiction that made her even more captivating.

She had an otherworldly charm that was hard to ignore. Her delicate features were framed by loose strands of hair that escaped the neat ponytail she wore. Her eyes, large and expressive, held a depth of emotion that spoke of experiences beyond her years. Despite the tiredness etched in her face, there was an inner strength that radiated from her, a quiet resilience that made her seem almost magical. She looked like a girl from a fairy tale, carrying a unique charm that set her apart.

"Mister, I asked you what you are doing with my file," she repeated, her voice now tinged with impatience.

"Sorry," I stammered, stumbling over my words. "I saw the ID card and it looked familiar. I didn't mean to pry. I was just curious."

She looked at me with narrowed eyes, clearly unimpressed. "So, you think a simple sorry will suffice for invading someone's privacy?"

I paused, feeling the heat rise to my cheeks. "I'm extremely sorry. I didn't mean any harm."

"So, what did you learn from looking into the file?" she pressed, her tone relentless.

"Nothing," I replied, my voice barely above a whisper.

"I asked you, what did you learn from the file?" she repeated, her eyes boring into mine.

"Your name is Aahana, and you are diagnosed with osteosarcoma," I said, my voice filled with regret.

Aahana sighed, her expression softening just a fraction. "So, you learned that much. Did you Google it?"

I nodded, feeling even more awkward under her scrutiny. "Yes, but I didn't get the chance to read much. You appeared before I could."

"Googling it, huh?" she said, a faint smile tugging at the corners of her lips. "Well, since you already know the basics, I might as well tell you the rest."

We began walking together, the hospital lobby bustling around us, creating a bubble of relative privacy in the midst of chaos. Her presence was calming, her demeanour unpretentious and straightforward.

"I have osteosarcoma," she explained, her voice steady. "It's a type of cancer that starts in the bones. In my case, the doctors gave me two options: endure severe pain and extend my life by about five years with chemo, or avoid chemo and have a shorter, more painless life."

Her words stunned me. I didn't know how to respond. Here she was, calmly discussing her limited options with a composed demeanour that belied the gravity of her situation.

"Both options have their flaws," she continued, her eyes distant as if looking into an uncertain future. "Living with pain for five years or living pain-free but shorter. I chose the latter option, thinking it's better to live without pain, even if it's shorter. So, I'm here for chemo."

I stared at her, speechless. The courage she displayed was beyond anything I could comprehend. Her strength, her acceptance of her fate, and her determination to live her life on her terms were awe-inspiring.

"Don't give me that look of regret," she said, noticing my expression. "I've seen it too many times. When I was diagnosed, I left behind close relatives and friends to avoid their pity."

"I'm sorry," I said, feeling utterly helpless, my words inadequate to express the depth of my empathy.

"Why are you here for chemo at this time?" I asked, trying to understand her situation better, my curiosity mingling with concern.

"I don't want anyone to know," she explained, her eyes meeting mine with a hint of defiance. "If I come here in the morning, someone might see me and figure it out. That's why I go to the office in the morning and come here late at night for treatment."

"Why didn't someone come with you?" I asked, concerned about her being alone.

"I and my mother are the only family I have. I don't want her to be with me every time I take chemo, so I asked her not to come," she replied, smiling slightly, a hint of pride in her independence. "If a girl comes alone late at night, people think it's because of work. But if she comes with her mother, they suspect something. So, I come alone."

"Isn't there better treatment for cancer abroad?" I asked, trying to offer some hope, my mind racing to find a solution for her.

"This cancer was diagnosed at a medical college," she explained, her tone pragmatic. "A research team is working on how to treat it. It's a rare kind of cancer, so there aren't many known causes or treatments. Until my time comes, I want to live happily without this tension."

I glanced at the time, feeling conflicted about having to leave for work, my heart heavy with the weight of our conversation.

"Do you need to go home?" she asked, noticing my concern, her eyes reflecting a mixture of understanding and detachment.

"No, I work the night shift," I explained, feeling a sudden urge to be there for her, to offer some form of support. "I need to go to the office."

"Alright, you should go," she said, her tone practical yet kind. "But don't worry about me. I come and go alone every day. I don't need anyone to accompany me."

"Can I walk you home? It's late for you to be alone," I offered, feeling protective, my concern overriding my usual reticence.

She shook her head, her expression resolute. "We just met. A few minutes ago, you didn't even know my name, and now you know my whole medical history. I told you because you already knew so much. Don't expect anything more from me."

"Okay," I said, feeling a mix of respect and helplessness, realizing the depth of her independence.

"We're just strangers," she concluded, her eyes reflecting a quiet strength. "We might never meet again. Goodbye."

"Goodbye," I replied, my voice tinged with regret, watching her walk away, her figure slowly fading into the night.

I headed to my Rapido ride which I booked earlier and rode to the office, As I rode through the quiet streets, I couldn't shake the image of her from my mind. What kind of person was she, to be dealing with something as severe as cancer with such grace and strength? The thought lingered with me, a reminder of the fleeting nature of life and the unexpected connections we make along the way.

My mind filled with thoughts of Aahana—a beautiful girl with a radiant smile, fighting a battle that chemo couldn't help. Her courage and determination left a lasting impression on me, stirring something deep within that I had long forgotten.

Shifting Perspectives

Gentle reminder for all the readers

From the upcoming chapter onwards, the narration will not be solely based on Surya's perspective. Instead, it will be presented from a third-party viewpoint, involving conversations between two people for the reader's sake.

CHAPTER VI

The Dream

Surya returned to his office and slumped into his chair, his head in his hands. The day's events replayed in his mind, leaving him overwhelmed with new and unsettling revelations. He had learned so much about things he never expected to know.

As he pondered, a colleague named Phani approached, engaged in a phone call. Ending the call, Phani sat down beside Surya, his expression concerned.

"Surya," Phani called softly, gradually increasing his volume, "Surya... Surya!"

"What is it?" Surya responded, finally snapping out of his thoughts.

"Shanti mentioned you fell earlier. What happened?" Phani asked with concern.

Surya showed him his hand, indicating the injury without elaborating. The bandage was already starting to loosen, revealing a fresh scrape underneath.

"How did that happen?" Phani pressed, his brow furrowing.

"It's nothing. Why did you come in late today?" Surya deflected, trying to change the subject.

"You know why," Phani replied, his tone serious.

"Bindu, huh?" Surya remarked, understanding dawning on him.

"Yeah," Phani confirmed with a sigh.

Surya's thoughts drifted back to the time when Phani and Bindu were the talk of the office. They had both joined Accenture as freshers, their paths crossing in the most unexpected yet predictable of ways. After that they both shifted to TCS together, and Surya can vividly remember the day they both joined the company.

Theirs was a love story that blossomed amidst shared projects and late-night brainstorming sessions, a connection that grew stronger with each passing day.

Surya remembered the subtle glances they exchanged during meetings, the way they always seemed to find reasons to collaborate on assignments. It wasn't long before their professional relationship turned personal. Their colleagues watched with a mix of envy and admiration as Phani and Bindu navigated the delicate balance of work and romance. Their love story reached its zenith when, against the backdrop of supportive friends and families, they decided to get married. It was a union blessed by their parents, a rare and beautiful culmination of both love and tradition.

However, life had a way of throwing curveballs. Not long after their wedding, Bindu received an irresistible career opportunity in Bangalore, one that promised growth and advancement she couldn't achieve by staying put. With heavy hearts but mutual understanding, they decided she should take the opportunity. Phani remained at the company, choosing stability over the uncertainty of a new city and a new job.

In the days that followed Bindu's departure, Phani's demeanor changed. Surya had initially assumed that Phani's quiet nature was simply a reflection of his own introversion. Phani was often seen alone, working diligently at his desk, rarely engaging in the office banter that others seemed to thrive on. He seemed content in his solitude, much like Surya, who valued the peace that came with being left to his own thoughts.

But as time went on, Surya began to notice the subtle signs of Phani's inner turmoil. The distant look in his eyes, the way he often stared at his phone, waiting for a message or a call that might bridge the distance between him and Bindu. It was then that Surya realized Phani's silence wasn't a choice; it was a consequence. The absence of Bindu had left a void in his life, one that no amount of work or distraction could fill.

Surya felt a pang of empathy for his colleague. He understood, in a way, the loneliness that came from missing someone dear. He saw in Phani a reflection of his own struggles with isolation and the yearning for a connection that seemed just out of reach. This shared experience, though unspoken, forged a silent bond between them.

As Surya sat there listening to the conversation of Phani, these memories of Phani and Bindu lingered in his mind. He couldn't help but think of how life's unexpected turns could shape a person's destiny, how love and loss could coexist, creating a complex tapestry of emotions that defined who they were. And as he stepped out into the early morning light, he felt a renewed sense of determination to face whatever the day had in store, drawing strength from the stories and experiences that connected them all.

"What's going on now?" Surya asked, bringing himself back to the present.

Phani's face fell. "It's not working out anymore. No matter how many chances we give, this relationship isn't getting better."

Surya reflected on this. It wasn't just physical distance separating them; their hearts were drifting apart too.

"You're already prepared to go to Bangalore. What's the problem now?" Surya queried.

"We both want to be together, but the reasons to stay together aren't enough anymore. The thought of separation brings us together, but staying together requires reasons we don't have," Phani explained, his voice heavy with emotion. "And right now, I don't have those reasons."

As Phani continued talking, Surya's mind wandered again, pondering why people strive to stay together when the connection is fading. He considered his own life, his relationships, and the mysterious girl he had met.

• • •

Later that evening, Surya returned home, unlocking the door with a spare key. He dropped his bag by the door and headed to the fridge for some water. The cool liquid soothed his parched throat as he leaned against the counter, lost in thought.

He glanced towards a door and walked over, opening it to reveal his uncle and aunt sleeping inside. They looked peaceful; their faces softened by the embrace of sleep. Surya felt a pang of gratitude for their presence in his life, a silent support system that had been there through thick and thin.

After a shower, Surya felt slightly refreshed but still mentally drained. He collapsed onto his bed. The soft mattress seemed to pull him in, offering a brief moment of comfort. He closed his eyes, hoping for sleep to take him quickly.

A few moments later, he heard the familiar creak of the door. Swecha, his cousin, entered the room silently. She moved with the quiet grace of someone who had done this many times before. Swecha had always cared deeply for Surya, ever since they were children.

Swecha gently covered Surya with a blanket, a small gesture of care that she performed nightly. It was her way of showing love and concern without words, as speaking about their feelings was something neither of them found easy.

Surya felt the blanket settle over him, knowing it was Swecha's doing. He kept his eyes closed, pretending to be asleep. He appreciated her silent care but chose not to acknowledge it openly. Surya was aware of her feelings and the comfort she tried to provide, but he was determined not to deepen any emotional bonds. He feared that acknowledging her care might complicate their already delicate relationship. He didn't want to foster any false hopes in Swecha or in himself. They both needed to heal in their own ways, without relying too heavily on each other for emotional support.

Swecha lingered for a moment, perhaps hoping for some sign of acknowledgment. But when none came, she quietly left the room, closing the door softly behind her. Surya lay still, his mind a swirl of conflicting emotions. He knew she cared deeply, and in a different time, under different circumstances, things might have been different between them. But now, he chose to maintain the distance.

His thoughts drifted back to Aahana, the girl he had met in the hospital. Her face, her diagnosis, the strange sense of connection he felt – everything about her intrigued and troubled him. The memory of her laughter and her resilience haunted him, filling his mind as he drifted into an uneasy sleep.

In the hazy landscape of his dream, Surya found himself back in the sterile, cold corridors of the hospital. The fluorescent lights flickered overhead, casting eerie shadows on the walls. The smell of antiseptic lingered in the air. He wandered aimlessly, the halls stretching endlessly before him, a maze he couldn't escape.

Then he saw her. Aahana stood at the end of the corridor, her face a mix of calm and pain. She looked more fragile than he remembered, her figure almost ethereal in the dim light. She smiled at him, the same serene smile that had captivated him, but there was a sadness in her eyes that he hadn't noticed before.

Surya tried to move towards her, but his feet felt heavy, as if glued to the floor. His heart raced with urgency and panic. Suddenly, out of the shadows, figures emerged, faceless and shrouded in darkness. They approached Aahana, and before Surya could react, they lifted her from the ground. Her expression turned to one of distress as they began to carry her away.

"Don't take her!" he yelled, desperation clawing at his throat. Aahana reached out a hand towards him, her eyes pleading for help. Surya pushed harder against the invisible force holding him back, his breath coming in ragged gasps. But no matter how hard he tried, he couldn't bridge the gap between them.

The dream began to blur, the edges of his vision darkening. Just as Aahana was about to disappear into the shadows, Surya jolted awake, his heart pounding. He sat up abruptly, drenched in sweat, his breath heavy and uneven. The room was dark and silent, the only sound the frantic beating of his own heart.

He ran a hand over his face, trying to shake off the remnants of the dream. The vividness of it left him unsettled. He couldn't understand why this girl, whom he had met only once, had such a profound impact on him. Her presence in his dream felt like a call for help, a plea that he couldn't ignore.

Surya lay back down, staring at the ceiling. Sleep seemed impossible now, his mind too active with thoughts of Aahana. He couldn't shake the feeling that she was in danger, that he needed to see her again. The dream had felt so real, her distress so palpable. He tried to dismiss the thought but felt an unease he couldn't shake.

"What was that?" he wondered aloud. "Why did she appear in my dream, being taken away by someone?"

• • •

The next day, Surya felt restless at his desk. To distract himself, he opened his phone and watched YouTube shorts. A video about a girl with a similar story to the one he'd learned of flashed on the screen, bringing the girl back to his mind. Glancing at the time, he saw it was 11:00 PM, the time she usually came for chemo.

Unable to ignore the nagging feeling, he decided to go to the hospital.

He waited where he had met her the previous night. The hospital lobby was eerily quiet, the dim lighting casting long shadows. His mind raced with negative thoughts, and he felt a mounting sense of dread. As his anxiety peaked, someone placed a hand on his shoulder. Surya spun around to see Aahana.

"You're here again," she observed, her expression a mix of surprise and curiosity.

He let out a sigh of relief as the cool night air seemed to calm his nerves. "I... I was worried about you," he stammered.

"Why? Did the doctor tell you to come back today, or is your hand hurting?" she asked, her concern evident.

"No, I came for you," he admitted.

"For me? What, did you come to offer sympathy?" she asked, her frustration evident.

"No, not at all," he insisted.

"Then why?" she pressed.

"Honestly, after I dreamed about you last night, I couldn't shake this uneasy feeling. I had to make sure you were okay," he explained.

"You dreamt about me? What kind of dream?" she asked, intrigued.

"I saw someone carrying you away," he said, his tone serious.

"Someone carrying me away? That's a bit dramatic, don't you think?" she chuckled, trying to lighten the mood.

"I'm not joking. It felt so real," he insisted.

"Look, I've been coming here for chemo for three months, and nothing like that has happened. People are still around when I leave, and I walk home without fear. Why are you so concerned after just one encounter?" she questioned.

Surya couldn't find the words to explain his feelings. "I don't know. Maybe it's because meeting you and learning about your fight made me realize how precious life is."

"It's getting late, and I have to be at the office in the morning," she said, preparing to leave.

"Let me drop you home," Surya offered.

"No, I prefer to walk. After chemo, lying down makes me uneasy. Walking helps me feel better, and I can sleep soundly afterward," she explained.

"Alright," Surya conceded, understanding her need for independence.

"Okay, goodbye. Don't worry about me; I'll be fine. Focus on your work," she said, starting to walk away.

Surya watched her go, his mind still restless. "Alright. Take care," he called after her.

Later, she opened her gate, and as the streetlights cast a warm glow at the corner of the street, Surya stepped out of the shadows, watching her until she was safely inside.

"Uff, I need to get to the office," he muttered to himself as he walked back to his bike and rode off into the night.

CHAPTER VII

Surya's Inner Struggle

Surya returned to the office and settled into his chair, feeling a newfound sense of peace. The office, with its typical open-plan layout, was filled with the soft hum of computers and the quiet murmur of colleagues conversing in hushed tones. Rows of desks lined up neatly under fluorescent lights, each workspace personalized with family photos, coffee mugs, and a scattering of papers. Motivational posters adorned the walls, and whiteboards filled with scribbled notes and flowcharts stood testament to the bustling activity that usually characterized their workspace.

The overwhelming worry that had gripped his heart for so long had finally loosened its hold. He knew now, with a clarity that had eluded him before, that Aahana was safe, and nothing catastrophic was going to happen to her. The oppressive weight of dread that had shadowed him seemed to lift, replaced by a serene calmness that felt almost foreign. He allowed himself to breathe deeply and fully, letting go of the tension that had coiled tightly within him. Leaning back in his chair, he closed his eyes for a moment and savoured the relief.

As he sat there reflecting, he came to an important realization. The thought of visiting Aahana day after day no longer felt like a burden or an obligation. Instead, it became a source of comfort and purpose. He welcomed the idea, finding a sense of stability and routine in knowing he would see her, talk to her, and be there for her. This brought him a sense of emotional equilibrium he desperately needed.

He understood now that it wasn't just about ensuring Aahana's well-being anymore. It was also about his own. He could live with the thought of Aahana being safe, and if visiting her daily was what it took to maintain that sense of security, then he was more than willing to do it. He was no longer haunted by the possibility of her being taken away from the hospital or by any other unforeseen tragedy. That dread had been replaced by a quiet determination to support her through whatever came next. And in doing so, he found he was also supporting himself, finding his own strength and resilience in the process.

Just then, Phani, his colleague and friend, approached his desk. Phani was a stocky man with a genial face, always ready with a smile or a joke to lighten the mood. Today, however, there was a look of concern on his face.

"Where did you go, Surya?" Phani asked, his voice tinged with curiosity.

"Nowhere. Did anyone ask about me?" Surya replied, trying to sound nonchalant.

"No, no one asked," Phani said, shaking his head. "Any server issues?" he added, shifting the conversation to work.

"No, everything's fine. The ticket you raised yesterday got resolved. Apart from that, no new developments," Surya replied, feeling a sense of relief that there were no pressing issues to deal with.

"Oh, okay," Phani said, nodding. Then, noticing the tired look on Surya's face, he asked, "Why do you look so exhausted?"

In the background, Surya remembered the events from the night. He had hurried from Aahana's house back to the hospital and then ridden his bike to the office. The memory was a blur of frantic movements and anxiety.

"Nothing," he replied, not wanting to delve into the details.

"So, what's the plan for this weekend? It's New Year, after all," Phani asked, trying to lift the mood.

"Nothing much. Just like every year, I'll stay at home," Surya said, shrugging.

Phani smiled slightly, a knowing look in his eyes.

"Why are you smiling? What more do you expect from me?" Surya asked, feeling a bit defensive.

"Nothing. If you have no plans, you could come over to my place. We could have a drink," Phani suggested, his tone friendly.

"Phani, I don't drink, and I don't like hanging out with people who do. Let's not bring up alcohol between us," Surya replied firmly.

Having history of alcoholic interference in his life Surya became so traumatised with alcohol and the addicts.

"Okay," Phani said, raising his hands in a gesture of surrender.

Surya completed his office hours and returned home. The sun was setting, casting long shadows across the city. He unlocked the main door, then his room door, followed by the bathroom door. After a quick shower, he collapsed onto his bed, exhaustion overtaking him. Later, when he woke up, he noticed a blanket over him. It was neatly tucked in, a small but telling gesture.

"Swecha, I told you not to take care of me. Do your own work and let me be. You know I can't reciprocate your feelings. Please understand that. No matter what you do, I can't return your feelings the way you want. Please understand," he thought to himself, feeling a pang of guilt and frustration.

"Nothing has changed. How can I make her understand?" he muttered to himself, feeling the weight of his unspoken words pressing heavily on his heart.

Surya woke up for his night shift and went to the office, settling back into his chair. The night was quiet, the office eerily silent with most of the staff gone. Surya leaned back in his chair, his thoughts turning inward as he stared absently at the papers on his desk. He couldn't ignore the tugging of his emotions anymore, and they led him straight to thoughts of Swecha.

"Swecha," he mused silently, a sigh escaping his lips. "I told you not to take care of me. You've always been so kind, so thoughtful, always putting my needs before your own. But you deserve better than this, better than me." He shook his head, a heavy feeling settling in his chest. He remembered all the times Swecha had been there for him, her unwavering support and understanding a balm to his troubled soul. Yet, despite her efforts, a wall remained between them—one he couldn't break down, no matter how much he wanted to ease her pain.

"Do your own work and let me be," he thought, a touch of bitterness creeping in. "You have so much potential, so many dreams. Don't tie yourself to someone who can't give you what you deserve." He could see her smiling face in his mind, her eyes always filled with hope and something deeper—something he couldn't mirror back.

"You know I can't reciprocate your feelings," he continued, his heart aching with the weight of the truth. "Please understand that." He wished things were different, that he could return her feelings with the same intensity she had for him. But his heart was elsewhere, entangled in memories and emotions he couldn't untangle.

"No matter what you do, I can't return your feelings the way you want," he admitted to himself, a lump forming in his throat. He hated seeing her hurt, hated the thought of being the cause of her pain. Yet, he knew leading her on would only make things worse.

"Please understand," he pleaded silently, his thoughts heavy with regret. "I don't want to be the one who dims your light." He closed his eyes, taking a deep breath, hoping that somehow, Swecha would find the strength to move on and find happiness elsewhere—happiness that he couldn't provide.

Surya opened his eyes, the burden of his unspoken words pressing heavily on his heart. He knew he needed to find a way to convey his feelings to Swecha, to make her understand without breaking her spirit. For now, he resolved to tread carefully, to find the right moment to let her know, hoping that in the end, she would find the love and joy she deserved.

Phani arrived on time to distract him from his disrupted thoughts. Phani was a punctual person, always arriving early to get a head start on the day's work.

"Hey, you seem like you've been here early," Phani said, raising an eyebrow.

"That's what I should ask you. Why are you here on time?" Surya replied, trying to deflect the attention.

"Nothing, bro," Phani said, shrugging.

"Did Bindu call you?" Surya asked.

"No," Phani replied, shaking his head.

"Have you thought about going to Bangalore to try to clear things up between you two?" Surya asked.

"Our problem isn't just the distance. It started with behaviour issues and now it's come to a point where she wants a divorce. Her father asked me to speak with their lawyer," Phani admitted, his voice tinged with sadness.

"Is it that serious?" Surya asked, his concern evident.

"Yeah," Phani said, forcing a smile.

"What's your plan now?" Surya asked.

"I don't know. A relationship needs two people to work together. If one gives up, it's hard to keep it going," Phani said, his voice resigned. "Bro, I can't say that this is how everyone's life turns out, but this is how my life has unfolded. Everyone's life is different. If a paperboy can become Abdul Kalam, another paperboy might remain just a paperboy. When their lives are not the same, why should our relationships end the same way despite both enduring their own struggles?"

Surya's thoughts delved deeper into the essence of human existence, the myriad paths each individual could take. He realized that while one person's journey could lead them to greatness, another might find themselves stuck in the same place, despite having started from similar circumstances.

"This divergence in life paths is what makes each person's story unique," he continued to ponder. He reflected on the relationships in his life, understanding that just as no two lives are identical, no two relationships are alike either. Each relationship carries its own set of challenges, triumphs, and lessons. Surya mused on the fact that the struggles he and Swecha faced were part of their unique journey. Even if their relationship didn't turn out the way Swecha hoped, it didn't mean it was any less significant or meaningful.

Surya realized that he needed to accept the differences in their journeys and acknowledge that their paths, though intertwined for a time, might lead them in different directions. "I have to respect our individual paths," he concluded. "Our struggles, our triumphs, they shape us into who we are. And maybe, just maybe, our relationship, with all its imperfections, is perfect in its own way."

With a deep sigh, Surya embraced the idea that life's unpredictability was what made it beautiful. The different paths people take, the varied outcomes of similar beginnings, and the unique essence of each relationship are what give life its rich tapestry of experiences. And in that tapestry, he found a sense of peace, knowing that every thread, every twist and turn, had its place.

"Why am I drifting into thoughts I never experienced?" Surya thought, shaking his head to clear it.

"I know you don't believe in relationships, Surya. But not all relationships are bad. Just because you had a bad experience doesn't mean they all are," Phani said, trying to offer some perspective.

Phani is trying to tell me something through his life. But I can't relate. People change, and relationships fall apart, Surya thought to himself.

Surya glanced at the clock. It was 12:00, and he was reminded of the hospital and Aahana.

"Bro, I need to step out for a bit. Call me if anything comes up," he said, standing up and grabbing his jacket.

As Surya walked out of the office, he felt a mixture of emotions—relief, determination, and a hint of sadness. The journey he was on was a complex one, filled with highs and lows, but he knew that each step he took was leading him towards a better understanding of himself and his place in the world.

CHAPTER VIII

The New Routine

Surya, after his deep and intense conversation with Phani, rode to the hospital with a heavy heart and a mind full of contemplative thoughts. The familiar rumble of his bike beneath him was a comforting constant, even as his mind swirled with confusion and contemplation. The streets were bathed in the soft, orange glow of streetlights, casting long shadows that seemed to echo the turmoil within him.

Parking his bike, he found himself lingering at a distance, his eyes fixed on the entrance of the hospital. The quiet of the evening seemed to wrap around him, amplifying the silence within his own mind. The hospital, a towering structure of concrete and glass, stood solemnly against the night sky, its entrance bustling with activity as doctors, nurses, and visitors moved in and out. He stood there, almost as if rooted to the spot, questioning his motives. "Why am I here?" he wondered, a mixture of confusion and curiosity swirling within him. The hospital doors seemed to hold a magnetic pull over him, drawing him closer with every passing second.

His mind replayed the conversation with Phani, the weight of those words still pressing heavily on his chest. It had been a conversation filled with truths and realizations, stirring up feelings he had long kept buried. As he stood there, the reality of his emotions began to dawn on him. The air was cool, with a slight breeze that carried the faint scent of antiseptic and blooming night flowers. The distant hum of city life served as a backdrop to his introspection, a reminder of the world moving on while he stood still.

"Why do I care if Aahana gets home safely?" he thought, struggling to understand his own actions. It wasn't just about stepping out of his comfort zone; it was about confronting the depths of his own feelings. Aahana had become more than just a passing acquaintance; she had carved out a place in his life that he couldn't easily ignore. The vulnerability he felt in that moment was new and unsettling. Surya was used to maintaining control, to keeping his emotions in check. But here he was, waiting in the dim light of the evening, driven by a concern he couldn't fully rationalize. "What is it about her that makes me do this?" he questioned himself, searching for answers in the stillness of the night.

As he stood there, the hospital entrance became a symbol of his inner conflict. On one hand, it represented his desire to protect and ensure Aahana's safety; on the other, it was a gateway to his own self-discovery. Every minute that passed heightened his awareness of the depth of his concern for her. Surya took a deep breath, feeling the cool night air fill his lungs. He realized that caring for someone, truly caring, often meant stepping into the unknown, embracing vulnerability, and acknowledging feelings that might not always make sense. It was in these moments of uncertainty that the true nature of his heart revealed itself.

As he watched people come and go through the hospital doors, Surya accepted that his presence there wasn't just about Aahana's safety. It was about his own journey of understanding his emotions, about breaking down the walls he had built around his heart. And in that acceptance, he found a strange sense of peace, ready to face whatever the night, and life, had in store for him.

Just as he was about to leave, thinking she might have already left the hospital, Aahana appeared. Her slender frame was silhouetted against the bright lights of the hospital entrance, and she walked with a grace that seemed to captivate everyone around her. Her eyes, though tired, sparkled with an inner strength and determination.

"Hey, my house is over there," she said, pointing in the direction of her home.

"You..." Surya started, his voice faltering as he tried to find the right words.

"You followed me home last night and then came back to the hospital today. What do you want?" she asked, her tone a mixture of curiosity and annoyance.

"Well, last night..." he began, struggling to explain his actions.

"You didn't need to follow me. Are you here to drop me home today?" she interrupted; her voice softer but still questioning.

"Hmm," he nodded, unsure of what else to say.

"You said you had night shifts. You've been here for three days straight. Didn't anyone ask you anything?" she asked, raising an eyebrow.

"No," he replied simply.

"Why do freshers always worry about what TLs think? We've got a guy in our team, Pradeep, who's married but still sucks up to the TL," she said, shaking her head with a slight smile.

Surya showed no expression, his mind too occupied with his own thoughts to respond.

"I have a headache. Can we get some coffee?" she asked, her tone now wearier than before.

"Sure," he replied.

They went to a nearby coffee shop, its warm, inviting atmosphere a stark contrast to the sterile, cold environment of the hospital. The soft murmur of conversations and the clinking of cups created a comforting background noise. They drank their coffee in silence, the rich aroma of freshly brewed coffee mingling with the quiet hum of the shop. The dim lighting cast a soft glow on their faces, highlighting the lines of fatigue and contemplation etched on both their features.

Surya dropped Aahana near her home. As she walked towards her gate, she turned back, her eyes meeting his with a questioning look.

"Should I wait for you tomorrow?" she asked, her voice filled with an unexpected hopefulness.

Surya paused, his heart pounding in his chest. "I'll be there," he replied, feeling a sense of commitment he couldn't quite understand.

As he started his bike, Surya thought to himself, "Why did I say that? I already came today; why am I going again tomorrow?" The thought lingered in his mind as he rode home, the cool night air whipping past him, mingling with the warmth of the coffee still in his system.

• • •

The next day, Surya went through his routine—getting up, getting ready, heading to the office. The familiar rhythm of his day provided a comforting predictability, even as his thoughts kept drifting back to Aahana. As soon as the clock struck 12:00, he left for the hospital.

Aahana was waiting for him, her posture relaxed but her eyes scanning the surroundings until they landed on him.

"Did your session end early?" he asked, a note of curiosity in his voice.

"No, it ended at 11:45 as usual," she replied, a small smile playing on her lips.

"But yesterday you didn't come out until 12," he said, his brows furrowing in confusion.

"Who said that? I came out and waited," she corrected him, her tone matter-of-fact.

"I didn't tell you I was coming," he said, puzzled by her actions.

"I had a feeling you would, so I waited," she replied, her eyes meeting his with an intensity that made his heart skip a beat.

"What if I didn't come?" he asked, genuinely curious.

"I would've just gone home," she said with a shrug, her nonchalance masking a deeper emotion.

"Oh," he replied, feeling a mixture of relief and confusion.

As Aahana got on the bike, she leaned closer to him, her presence a comforting weight against his back.

"Want some coffee?" he asked, hoping to prolong their time together.

"No," she replied, her voice soft but firm.

"Okay, if you need anything, let me know," he said, feeling a strange need to take care of her.

"I don't need anything, but I do have a doubt. Why are you doing this for me?" she asked, her tone filled with genuine curiosity.

"Do you want the truth?" he asked, his heart pounding in his chest.

"Yes," she replied, her eyes searching his face for answers.

"After I met you, I had a dream where someone was harassing you. I wanted to make sure you were safe, so I followed you home," he confessed, his voice barely above a whisper.

"Do you think someone will really harass me?" she asked, her eyes wide with surprise.

"No, but I wanted to be sure," he admitted, feeling a weight lift off his shoulders as he spoke.

"Okay, drop me off then," she said, her voice softer, almost touched by his concern.

As they reached her home, she looked back, her eyes meeting his once again.

"Wait for me tomorrow?" she asked, a small smile playing on her lips.

"Sure," he replied, feeling a sense of warmth spread through him.

Surya thought to himself, "Why did I agree again? Why am I going out of my way for her?" He returned to the office, lost in his thoughts, the day's events replaying in his mind. As he settled back into his routine, he realized that sometimes, the heart has reasons that reason cannot understand.

• • •

The next evening, Surya found himself at the hospital entrance once more, his heart pounding in anticipation. Aahana appeared, her presence like a beacon in the dimly lit surroundings. They greeted each other with a familiarity that had grown between them, a silent understanding that words could not fully capture.

"Want to grab an ice cream?" Aahana suggested, her eyes twinkling with a hint of mischief.

"Sure," Surya replied.

They walked to a nearby ice cream cart, the vendor's cheerful face a welcome sight. The cart was a colourful, vibrant contrast to the monotony of the hospital surroundings, with a variety of Flavors displayed in bright, inviting colours. The scent of freshly made waffle cones wafted through the air, mingling with the sweet aroma of the ice cream.

As they enjoyed their ice creams, Surya couldn't help but feel a sense of contentment. The simplicity of the moment, the shared laughter, and the comfort of each other's presence created a bubble of warmth around them. They talked about their days, their dreams, and their fears, each conversation peeling back another layer of their personalities.

After finishing their ice creams, Aahana suggested, "How about exploring DLF tonight? I've heard the nightlife there is amazing."

"Let's do it," Surya agreed, his curiosity piqued.

They rode to DLF, the bustling energy of the place enveloping them as soon as they arrived. The streets were alive with activity, the neon lights of shops and restaurants casting a vibrant glow on the surroundings. The sound of music, laughter, and chatter filled the air, creating a lively, electric atmosphere.

They wandered through the streets, exploring the various food stalls and shops. They tried different street foods, from spicy chats to delicious momos, each bite a new adventure for their taste buds. They even found a small, cozy café that served the best coffee and pastries, the perfect place to rest and soak in the lively ambiance.

As the night progressed, they stumbled upon a street performer, his guitar music drawing a small crowd. They stood there, captivated by the soulful tunes and the passion with which the performer played. It was a magical moment, the music weaving a spell that seemed to bind them closer together.

By the end of the night, they had created a new routine, one that involved exploring the city's hidden gems, sharing ice creams, and discovering new places together. Each evening became an adventure, a journey of self-discovery and deepening connection. The hospital, the coffee shop, the ice cream cart, and DLF became landmarks in their shared memories, each place holding a special significance in their growing bond.

Surya realized that this new routine was more than just a way to spend time together; it was a path to understanding himself. The walls he had built around his heart were slowly crumbling, replaced by a sense of vulnerability and openness. And in that vulnerability, he found a strength he had never known, a strength that came from caring deeply for someone and being willing to embrace the uncertainty of emotions.

As they said goodnight, Aahana's eyes met his, her gaze filled with warmth and affection. "See you tomorrow?" she asked, her voice hopeful.

"See you tomorrow," Surya replied, his heart full of a new, unspoken promise.

As he rode home, the cool night air whipping past him, Surya couldn't help but smile. This new routine, with all its unpredictability and excitement, had become a journey of self-discovery and connection. And in that journey, he found a sense of purpose and joy that made every moment worthwhile.

CHAPTER IX

Ahana's Wish

The next day, Surya walked over to Phani's desk, a sense of determination settling in his chest. The office was buzzing with the usual hum of activity, the clatter of keyboards, and the muted conversations of coworkers. Surya's mind, however, was focused on one thing: his promise to Ahana.

"Phani garu, I'm stepping out for a bit," Surya said, his voice steady.

Phani looked up from his work, curiosity etched in the lines of his face. "Alright, take care," he responded, his tone carrying a hint of concern.

Surya left the office, heading towards the hospital, the familiar route becoming a part of his daily routine. The streets were bustling with evening traffic, the sky painted in hues of orange and pink as the sun began its descent. As he approached the hospital, he saw Ahana waiting for him, her figure framed by the harsh fluorescent lights of the entrance. Her eyes, though tired, lit up when she saw him.

"How long have you been out?" he asked, noticing the faint dark circles under her eyes.

"Do you have any work?" she responded, deflecting his concern with a question of her own.

Surya hesitated for a moment. "Are you hungry?"

Ahana's lips curled into a small smile. "Hungry means just dinner?"

Surya's brow furrowed in confusion. "Why? Do you need something else?"

Ahana's smile widened, a playful glint in her eyes. "Ice cream."

Surya chuckled softly, shaking his head. "I have a doubt. Can you eat right after therapy?"

Ahana's expression softened. "You can eat anything. There are no specific restrictions. We don't have much time anyway; if you feel like eating, just eat."

Surya fell silent, feeling a pang of sadness. The brevity of their time together, underscored by her casual acceptance, weighed heavily on him.

"Don't be senti, feel bad later. Let's go to Naturals," she suggested, her tone lightening the mood.

Surya's eyes widened slightly. "Do we need to go to Jubilee Hills now?"

Ahana raised an eyebrow, a mischievous glint in her eyes. "Will you take me there, or should I book a Rapido?"

Surya smiled, shaking his head. "I'll take you."

Ahana's face brightened, her smile genuine. "Okay, let's go."

The ride to Naturals was filled with a comfortable silence, both lost in their thoughts. The ice cream parlour was buzzing with life, families, friends, and couples chatted animatedly, their laughter and conversations blending into a comforting hum. The air was filled with the sweet scent of various ice cream flavours.

"I want a scoop of tender coconut and a scoop of sitaphal in one bowl," Ahana said, her eyes scanning the menu with interest.

"Alright," Surya nodded, heading to the counter to place their order.

A few moments later, Surya returned with the ice cream, handing the bowl to Ahana. "I didn't expect so many people to be here at this time," he remarked, looking around at the bustling crowd.

"Is this your first time coming here at this hour?" Ahana asked, a teasing smile playing on her lips.

Surya nodded. "First time at this time."

"Really? People stay like this for at least another half hour. Let's sit on that footpath," she suggested, pointing to a quieter spot just outside the parlour.

"Alright," Surya agreed, following her lead.

They sat down on the footpath, the cool night air providing a pleasant contrast to the warm atmosphere of the ice cream parlour. The city lights cast a gentle glow on their faces, illuminating the quiet intimacy of the moment.

"So, tell me," Ahana said, breaking the comfortable silence.

Surya looked at her, puzzled. "Tell you what?"

"I shared my top secret with you. Now, it's your turn," she said, her eyes twinkling with curiosity.

Surya hesitated, unsure of what to share. "I don't have any secrets."

Ahana shook her head, a knowing smile on her lips. "Everyone has things they prefer not to share with others. Those are secrets. People without them don't exist."

Surya sighed, realizing she wouldn't let it go. "My secrets aren't exciting."

"How do you know until you share them with me?" she countered; her gaze unwavering.

"Okay," Surya conceded, taking a deep breath.

"Summarize your life's important events, then elaborate on something interesting." Aahana said

Surya nodded, collecting his thoughts. "Born in BVRM, lost my parents early, raised by my uncle. Schooling in Bhimavaram, inter at Bhimavaram, college at Hyderabad, first job at TCS, now you know the rest."

Ahana frowned slightly, shaking her head. "You summarized your resume, not your life."

Surya chuckled softly. "My life isn't special."

"How about love?" Ahana asked, her tone softening.

Surya smiled slightly, looking to the side. "So, there was someone?"

"Not love, just a crush in tenth grade," he admitted, his voice tinged with nostalgia.

"Who? What's her name? Where is she now?" Ahana asked, her curiosity piqued.

"I'll tell you slowly. Her name was Anshu. Only I knew about my feelings; no one else did. Maybe she didn't even know I existed," Surya confessed, a wistful smile on his lips.

"How sad," Ahana murmured, her eyes softening with empathy.

"Most introverted one-sided love stories are like that," Surya said, a hint of resignation in his voice.

"Oh... one-sided love, huh?" Ahana echoed, her voice filled with understanding.

Surya glanced at his empty bowl, then back at Ahana. "I have completed my ice cream. Shall we go?"

Ahana nodded, a playful glint in her eyes. "Okay."

Surya dropped her off near her house, watching as she walked up to her gate, her steps light and graceful. He then went back to the office, his mind filled with thoughts of their conversation. Days passed, and their routine continued at the hospital. People around Surya noticed them and began to grow suspicious of their relationship.

One day, after her chemotherapy session, Ahana suggested they have coffee. They sat in a quiet corner of a nearby café, the warm, cozy atmosphere a welcome reprieve from the cold sterility of the hospital. The scent of freshly brewed coffee mingled with the soft murmur of conversations, creating a comforting backdrop to their conversation.

"I want to visit Annavaram Temple," she said, her voice soft but determined.

Surya looked at her, surprised. "When?"

"Next weekend," Ahana replied, her eyes reflecting a deep-seated longing.

Surya hesitated, thinking about his work schedule. "Who all are going?"

"Just you and me," Ahana said, her tone matter-of-fact.

Surya raised an eyebrow. "I didn't agree to come."

Ahana smiled, her eyes twinkling with mischief. "Come on, you would never let me go alone."

Surya sighed, knowing she was right. "I have work."

Ahana's smile faded slightly, replaced by a look of determination. "Fine, I'll manage."

Surya sighed deeply, knowing he couldn't let her go alone. "Shhh, okay, let's go. What will you tell at home?"

Ahana's face brightened instantly. "I already said I'm going with you."

Surya's eyes widened in surprise. "You mentioned me?"

"Yes," Ahana replied, her tone casual.

Surya shook his head in disbelief. "Fine, I'll borrow my colleague's car."

Ahana shook her head, a mischievous smile on her lips. "I already booked train tickets."

Surya's brow furrowed in confusion. "According to my memory, there's no direct train, right? Where did you book from?"

Ahana's eyes sparkled with excitement. "From here, we take a bus to BVRM, then catch the night train from there."

Surya sighed, a smile tugging at the corners of his lips. "We could drive."

Ahana shook her head, her excitement undiminished. "I want to take the train."

Surya chuckled softly, shaking his head in resignation. "Okay, okay."

As they sat there, sipping their coffee, Surya couldn't help but reflect on how much Ahana had come to mean to him. The walls he had built around his heart were slowly crumbling, and he found himself caring more deeply than he ever thought possible. The journey to Annavaram Temple seemed like more than just a trip; it felt like a step towards understanding his own heart.

CHAPTER X

The Sneak Out

Surya agreed to go with Ahana, and as the days passed, the trip to Annavaram approached. With the New Year around the corner, their routine continued: he would go to the hospital and drive her home every single day, including weekends. Days passed like a breeze, the familiarity of their interactions becoming a source of comfort for both.

A few days later, Surya went to the hospital but didn't find her there. His heart sank. However, as he walked through the familiar corridors and peered into the waiting room, she was nowhere to be found. His heart sank with a thud. He thought that she might already left to her home but he somewhat had mixed feeling about the situation.

Feeling a wave of panic rising within him, Surya quickly pulled out his phone and called her number. He listened intently as the line rang, but there was no answer. He tried again, his fingers trembling slightly as he redialled. Still no response. His concern grew with each passing second, a cold dread creeping into his chest.

Determined to find out what was going on, Surya drove to her home. The drive felt longer than usual, his mind racing with countless scenarios. When he finally arrived, he hurried to the front door, only to find it locked. He knocked, first gently, then more urgently, but there was no response from within. The house was eerily silent, the stillness amplifying his anxiety.

Surya's mind raced as he thought about all the possibilities. He tried to convince himself that they might have gone to visit relatives or perhaps taken a short trip to get away from the stress of the hospital. But deep down, a gnawing fear consumed him—the thought that Aahana's cancer might have taken a turn for the worse.

His breathing became heavier and more irregular as he stood there, staring at the locked door. The unease was palpable, each breath feeling like an effort. His thoughts spiralled, imagining the worst-case scenarios. What if she was in critical condition? What if something had happened and no one had informed him?

He took a deep breath, trying to steady himself, but the fear was relentless. It clawed at his insides, making it hard to think clearly. The connection he felt with Aahana was undeniable, and the thought of losing her or not being there when she needed support was unbearable.

In that moment, Surya resolved to do whatever it took to find her and make sure she was safe. He couldn't bear the uncertainty any longer. With a renewed sense of determination, he went to his bike, ready to visit the hospital again, contact her relatives, or do anything else necessary to ensure Aahana was alright.

Then all of a sudden. Surya realized he was not just out of his comfort zone; he had ventured much deeper into caring for Ahana than he had ever intended. With all these thoughts swirling in his mind, he tried to reassure himself, saying, "All is well. She will call me in the morning, I guess." But the thoughts wouldn't leave him. He went to the office, unable to brush off the worry.

After he reached the office, he went straight to his cubicle. He still can't brush of the feeling he had towards Aahana condition.

He started to recall the times they spent together, each memory amplifying his concern. Her laughter, her strength, the way she spoke about life with a nonchalance that belied her condition—all these moments played in his mind like a loop. He called her again, hearing the same ringing but no reply. The situation was unbearable.

After he completed his office hours, he wants to make sure whether she is at her house or not. So he went back to her house, still locked. He returned home, feeling helpless. The thoughts of her condition and her whereabouts tormented him, making sleep impossible.

At 8 PM the next day, his phone finally rang. It was Ahana.

"Hello, Ahana! Where are you? Is everything alright?" he asked, his voice trembling with concern.

"Hey, Surya. Sorry for making you worry. I had to go to the hospital suddenly for a new round of tests. My phone died, and I couldn't inform you," she explained calmly, her voice a soothing balm to his frazzled nerves.

Surya felt a wave of relief wash over him but also a pang of frustration. "You should have told me! I was so worried," he said, trying to keep his voice steady.

"But I am at hospital last night why can't I find you near the hospital," he said, with a doubt.

"I am admitted inside the patient lounge in hospital, so I think you have no reason to look for me in the patient room" Ahana replied.

"Next time you make sure to inform me" Surya insisted.

"I know, and I'm sorry. It all happened so fast. The doctors needed to run some urgent tests," Ahana replied.

"Are you okay now?" Surya asked, still anxious, the weight of his concern evident in his voice.

"Yes, I'm fine. They just wanted to make sure everything is under control. I'll be discharged tomorrow morning," she assured him, her tone soft and reassuring.

"It's okay. Just take care of yourself," Surya replied, feeling a mix of relief and exhaustion.

"Thank you, Surya. And again, I'm sorry for the worry," Ahana said, her voice softer, almost vulnerable.

"Alright. I'll pick you up in the morning," Surya said, finally able to breathe easier.

Surya sighed with a mixture of relief and mild exasperation. "I'll pick you up in the morning then."

But Ahana's voice remained firm. "I called you for the same reason. Have you forgotten that our bus to BVRM is today?"

Surya, feeling the weight of the day's events, tried to reason with her. "Ahana, your condition isn't good. We can go after a few days when you're feeling better."

"I don't know about that," she replied, her tone unwavering. "I'm going. If you want to join me, join me. I don't care whether you come or not."

Surya felt a surge of frustration but also understood her determination. "You said you'll be discharged tomorrow. We can start in the morning and still reach the train to Annavaram by night. Why should we go now?"

Ahana was resolute. "When I plan something, it should go as planned. If not, I get bad vibes. Just come, and we'll take the bus and reach BVRM by 4AM in the morning. I've booked a double bedroom for both of us at a hotel. We'll stay there and take the evening train."

Surya hesitated. "Why a hotel? I have a house there. We can stay for the night."

Ahana's voice softened but remained firm. "You said there's no one at your house. Do you expect me to clean the house just to stay for the day?"

Surya knew she was right. He sighed, a mix of frustration and understanding in his voice. "Okay, then. I'll pack my bag and meet you at the hospital."

Surya hung up the phone and took a moment to gather his thoughts. He realized how much Ahana's presence and determination had begun to affect him. Despite the whirlwind of emotions, he knew he couldn't let her go alone.

Back at his apartment, Surya quickly packed his essentials, throwing in clothes, toiletries, and a few personal items. As he zipped up his bag, his thoughts raced back to Ahana. Her determination, despite her condition, was something he admired, even if it frustrated him at times.

As he drove to the hospital, he couldn't shake off the feeling of unease. He parked his bike and walked briskly to the entrance, spotting Ahana waiting for him by the window. Her frail figure seemed smaller against the backdrop of the hospital, but her eyes sparkled with an unyielding resolve.

She looked up as he approached, a faint smile playing on her lips. "Ready?" she asked, her voice tinged with excitement.

Surya nodded, his resolve solidifying. "Ready."

• • •

Ahana had planned their escape meticulously. With a mischievous grin, she handed Surya a doctor's coat. "Put this on," she instructed, her eyes gleaming with excitement.

"Why should I wear this" Surya questioned.

"We are sneaking out from this hospital, if doctors find out you can say goodbye to our trip" Ahana answered.

"Then why exactly we are doing this" Surya asked.

"Do what I say," Ahana replied.

Surya raised an eyebrow but complied. "And what about you?"

Ahana pointed to a nurse's uniform draped over a nearby chair. "I'll wear this. We'll blend in and walk out like we belong."

Surya couldn't help but chuckle at the audacity of her plan. "You really thought this through, didn't you?"

Ahana nodded, her smile widening. "Absolutely. Let's go."

They navigated through the hospital corridors, their disguises giving them a sense of confidence. As they passed by nurses and doctors, Surya felt a thrill of excitement mixed with anxiety. The hospital's usual hum of activity seemed to fade into the background as they made their way to the exit.

Once outside, they quickly changed back into their regular clothes, stashing the disguises in a bag. Ahana's laughter filled the air, a sound that lightened Surya's heart. They hailed a cab and headed to the bus station, the thrill of their successful escape adding a sense of adventure to their journey.

• • •

They made their way to the bus station, the city lights flickering around them as they moved through the streets. The bus ride to BVRM was quiet, both lost in their thoughts. Ahana leaned her head against the window, her eyes closed, while Surya watched her, concern etched on his face.

By the time they reached BVRM, they were completely exhausted. The town, familiar to Surya, had a comforting air about it. They checked into the hotel; the room was simple but comfortable, a small sanctuary from the chaos of their journey. Ahana immediately settled in, looking exhausted.

Surya watched her, a mix of emotions swirling within him. "Get some rest," he said softly. "We'll head to the train station later."

Ahana nodded, her eyes heavy with sleep. "Thanks for coming," she murmured before drifting off. She found comfort in the bed and within seconds, she slipped into a sound sleep.

Surya sat beside her, the events of the past few days weighing on him. He realized that his feelings for Ahana had grown deeper than he had ever intended. Her strength and determination, even in the face of her illness, had touched him in ways he couldn't fully understand.

The entire day after seems like a night because both of them have slept all day only wake up to have brunch.

As the evening approached, they made their way to the train station. The station was bustling with activity, the air filled with the sounds of announcements and the distant hum of conversations. The journey to Annavaram awaited them, a trip that Surya never knew would be more than just a physical journey. It was a journey of emotions, realizations, and a deepening bond that neither of them had fully anticipated.

The rhythmic sound of the train chugging along filled the air as Surya and Ahana sat in their seats, quietly absorbing the surroundings. The train compartment was a mix of different people, each with their own stories and destinations.

***

Anshu borded the same train

Suddenly, another girl, Anshu, hurriedly entered the railway station, her eyes scanning the area. She quickly located her block and made her way to her assigned seat. As she settled in, she glanced across and saw the seat in front of her.

Anshu placed her bag on the overhead rack and took out her phone to make a call. "I boarded the train, so don't worry, Ma," she said, her voice a blend of relief and anticipation.

Surya, lost in thought, didn't notice Anshu at first. His mind was occupied with the journey ahead and the concern for Ahana. But as the train started moving, he couldn't help but feel a sense of connection to everyone around him, each person a part of the larger tapestry of life.

Ahana, sensing his unease, reached out and placed a hand on his. "We'll get through this, Surya," she said softly, her eyes conveying a depth of understanding and determination.

Surya looked at her, the strength in her gaze giving him a sense of calm. "I know," he replied, squeezing her hand gently.

As the train continued its journey, the two of them sat together, united by a bond that had grown stronger with each passing day. The road ahead was uncertain, but for the moment, they found solace in each other's company, ready to face whatever challenges lay ahead.

CHAPTER XI

Anshu's Narrative

Anshu sat by the window, gazing at the passing scenery, lost in a whirlwind of thoughts and emotions. The rhythmic sound of the train wheels clacking against the tracks served as a soothing backdrop as she drifted into memories of recent events that had significantly impacted her life.

• • •

The memory of her phone call with Harsha was vivid. She had quietly made her way to the terrace, seeking a moment of solitude amidst the chaos of her home. The cool evening breeze greeted her as she dialled Harsha's number. Harsha was the man her family had arranged for her to marry, and remarkably, in the short span of their first meeting, they had hit it off better than she could have ever anticipated.

As she listened to the dial tone, her mind wandered back to that eventful day. The marriage alliance meeting was a whirlwind of emotions, filled with a mixture of excitement, nervousness, and drama. It all happened so fast, within just ten minutes, yet it felt like a lifetime of decisions was made in that brief encounter.

She remembered walking into the room, her heart pounding with uncertainty, each beat echoing like a drum in her ears. The living room was meticulously decorated, with fresh flowers adorning the tables, their vibrant colours adding life to the space. The aroma of incense filled the air, a blend of sandalwood and jasmine that was both soothing and invigorating. It was clear that her parents had gone to great lengths to create a welcoming atmosphere for this meeting.

Her parents had painted a glowing picture of Harsha, extolling his virtues and accomplishments, but she couldn't help but feel sceptical. The concept of an arranged marriage had always seemed antiquated to her, a relic of a bygone era. Could such a tradition truly lead to happiness? She wasn't sure, and the doubts gnawed at her as she stepped further into the room.

However, all her doubts started to dissipate the moment she met him. Harsha stood up from the elegant sofa to greet her, his warm smile immediately putting her at ease. He was tall, with a calm and composed demeanour that radiated a sense of confidence. Yet, there was nothing arrogant or overbearing about him. His eyes were kind, reflecting a depth of understanding, and his voice, when he spoke, had a soothing quality that made her feel instantly comfortable.

The initial small talk, which she had dreaded, quickly blossomed into a deeper conversation. They discussed their favourite books, each recommendation turning into a lively discussion. He spoke passionately about his travels, sharing stories that transported her to distant lands. It was surprising how effortlessly they connected, as if they had known each other for years. She found herself laughing at his witty anecdotes, her laughter mingling with his, creating a harmonious symphony that filled the room.

The conversation was so engaging that they both lost track of time. They moved from one topic to another, the flow of dialogue as natural as a river's current. They shared stories from their childhoods, their aspirations, and even indulged in light-hearted banter that made her feel like she was chatting with an old friend rather than someone she had just met. Anshu was particularly impressed by Harsha's ability to listen attentively. He didn't just hear her words; he absorbed them, his thoughtful responses reflecting a genuine interest in her opinions and experiences. It was a quality she valued immensely, and his attentiveness made her feel respected and understood.

As they continued talking, the initial nerves and scepticism melted away, replaced by a growing sense of ease and comfort. Anshu realized that Harsha was not just a potential match arranged by their families but someone she could genuinely see herself building a future with. The compatibility between them was undeniable, each shared interest and common value adding another layer to the foundation of their connection.

By the end of their conversation, she felt a sense of hope and excitement for what lay ahead. Harsha wasn't just a figure in an arranged marriage scenario; he was a person she could envision sharing her life with. As they said their goodbyes, the warmth of his smile and the sincerity in his eyes lingered with her, filling her with a renewed belief in the possibilities that the future held.

• • •

Her thoughts were interrupted as Harsha answered the phone. His familiar voice brought a smile to her face.

"Hi Harsha," she greeted him, her voice filled with warmth.

"Hi Anshu," he replied, his tone equally warm. "How are you?"

"I'm good. Just needed to talk to you. A lot has been going through my mind since our meeting," she confessed.

"Same here," Harsha admitted. "It was quite an eventful day, wasn't it?"

Anshu laughed softly. "Eventful is an understatement. I never expected to feel so comfortable with you so quickly."

"I felt the same way," Harsha agreed. "I was prepared for it to be awkward, but it was anything but. It's like we clicked right from the start."

"Exactly," Anshu said, feeling a sense of relief that he felt the same way. "I keep thinking about how compatible we seemed. It's almost uncanny."

Harsha chuckled. "I know, right? It feels like we have known each other for much longer than just one meeting."

Anshu took a deep breath, her voice becoming more serious. "Harsha, I have something to tell you."

Harsha's tone shifted to a playful tease. "Let me guess, you're calling off our engagement?"

Anshu laughed, shaking her head. "As if I'd let you off the hook that easily!"

Harsha chuckled. "Alright, alright. What's up?"

Anshu hesitated for a moment, then decided to share her plans. "Nothing serious. I'm just going on a little trip."

Harsha's curiosity was piqued. "Where to?"

Anshu smiled. "It's not a bachelor party, don't worry. My mom wants us to visit Annavaram Satyanarayana Swami Temple for a special blessing before our engagement."

Harsha's interest grew. "Who's 'us?"

Anshu playfully replied, "Me and my boyfriend."

Harsha laughed. "Sorry, I'm really busy right now. I won't be able to join."

Anshu rolled her eyes, still smiling. "Nobody asked you to come, silly. I'm going with someone else."

Harsha's voice softened. "Oh, really? Who?"

Anshu's tone turned teasing. "Satyanarayana Garu. You know, your uncle."

Harsha laughed heartily. "Seriously, why are you telling me all this?"

Anshu's voice took on a mock serious tone. "According to the 'marriage rulebook' we wrote, I have to inform you of my whereabouts since our engagement. So, here I am, following the rules."

Harsha smiled; his voice warm. "Alright, be careful and take care of aunt and uncle. Let me know if you need anything."

Anshu's heart swelled with affection. "Will do. Thanks, soon-to-be Mr. Responsible!"

There was a moment of comfortable silence between them, each lost in their thoughts. Then Harsha spoke again, his voice more serious. "Anshu, I want you to know that I'm really looking forward to getting to know you better. Our first meeting was just the beginning, and I believe we have a lot to explore together."

Anshu's heart swelled with gratitude. "Thank you, Harsha. That means a lot to me. I feel the same way. I'm excited about our future and what it holds for us."

They talked for a while longer, discussing their plans and dreams, their hopes and fears. The conversation flowed naturally, reinforcing the connection they had felt during their first meeting. By the time they hung up, Anshu felt a renewed sense of optimism.

As she stood on the terrace, looking out at the night sky, she couldn't help but smile. Life had thrown a lot at her in a short span of time, but amidst the chaos, she had found something truly special. Harsha was more than just an arranged match; he was a promising partner; someone she could envision sharing her life with.

• • •

With a soft chuckle, Anshu ended the call and made her way back into the house. She was greeted by the sight of her parents in the middle of a heated discussion. The tension in the room was palpable.

Anshu's mother, her frustration evident, spoke up, "I've already booked the tickets. I've been telling you for so long that I want to have the first Subhaleka ceremony at the temple. How can I manage everything alone now?"

Anshu's father, with a sigh, replied, "Yes, you have mentioned it. But there are always some excuses. What can I do? You and Anshu should go."

Anshu's mother: "How can we leave all the wedding preparations here and go? There's so much to do."

Anshu interjected, "Both of you, stop arguing. No one else is coming. I'll go and come back soon."

Anshu's mother, worried: "You can't go alone. Either go with your father, or it doesn't matter. But you should not go alone."

Anshu's father: "Why are you making a big deal out of this? She can manage by herself."

Anshu's mother, insistent: "You seriously think it's okay to send her alone on such a long journey?"

Anshu's father: "What's the problem? If she can handle it, let her go."

Anshu's mother, finally relenting but still concerned: "Fine, do whatever you want. Just make sure to stay safe."

Anshu nodded, understanding her parents' concern but determined to make the trip. She reassured them both, "Don't worry, I'll be fine. I'll call you once I reach."

Anshu's mother sighed deeply but agreed, "Alright, just be careful and come back soon."

Anshu hugged her mother, grateful for her understanding. She then turned to her father and gave him a reassuring smile before heading towards the train.

• • •

The present moment on the train brought Anshu back to reality. She felt a mix of excitement and anticipation for the journey ahead. She leaned back in her seat, glancing around the compartment, taking in the sights and sounds of the bustling train station as it slowly began to fade into the distance.

Anshu's thoughts wandered to her parents, reflecting on the bond they shared. Her mother, always the worrier, fussed over every detail, wanting everything to be perfect for her daughter's big day. Anshu knew her mother's concern came from a place of deep love and care. Her father, on the other hand, was more pragmatic, believing in Anshu's independence and strength. He had always encouraged her to take on challenges head-on, trusting her judgment.

Their contrasting perspectives often led to disagreements, but Anshu appreciated how they balanced each other out. Her mother's emotional warmth and her father's rational support had shaped her into who she was. She felt a surge of gratitude for their unwavering support and love.

Anshu allowed herself to relax, feeling a sense of peace wash over her. She thought about the upcoming ceremony and the significance it held. Visiting the temple for a blessing before the engagement was not just a ritual; it was a moment to seek divine guidance and reassurance for the journey she was about to embark on with Harsha.

As the train moved steadily forward, Anshu closed her eyes, letting the rhythmic motion lull her into a state of calm. She thought about Harsha, their conversations, and the budding relationship that filled her with hope. She knew the road ahead would have its challenges, but with Harsha by her side, she felt ready to face anything.

The future was a vast, uncharted territory, but Anshu felt a newfound confidence. The journey to Annavaram was just the beginning, a symbolic step towards embracing the unknown with an open heart and mind. She smiled to herself, feeling the thrill of anticipation and the warmth of love that surrounded her.

The train's rhythmic chugging sound resumed, and with it, the promise of new beginnings and unexpected adventures filled the air. As Anshu settled into her seat, she couldn't help but feel that this trip to Annavaram was more than just a visit to a temple; it was a journey towards a new chapter in her life, one filled with hope, promise, and the thrilling uncertainty of what lay ahead.

As the train chugged along, Anshu drifted into a peaceful reverie, her thoughts a harmonious blend of past memories and future dreams. The journey had begun, and she was ready to embrace whatever lay ahead, knowing that she was not alone.

CHAPTER XII

The Reunion

Anshu sat in her seat, watching the scenery pass by. Verdant fields and distant hills rolled along as the train sped forward. The rhythmic clatter of the wheels against the tracks had a soothing effect, lulling her into a state of contemplation. A few rows ahead, Surya and Aahana took their seats. Anshu glanced at Surya, noticing a familiarity that she couldn't quite place. Curiosity piqued, she pulled out her phone and opened her school group chat. Scrolling through the profile pictures, she found the one that matched her memory and confirmed her suspicion. Heart pounding with excitement and nostalgia, she called out his name.

"Surya?"

Surya looked up, momentarily surprised. He told his companion to wait a moment and walked over to Anshu, a smile spreading across his face as recognition dawned.

Surya's mind raced back to his tenth-grade year, the last day of their social studies exam. He remembered the overwhelming sense of relief mixed with the anticipation of what lay ahead. That day was etched deeply into his memory. He had just finished the exam and was waiting for the bus, then comes Anshu surrounded by friends, when He saw Anshu standing a little distance away, looking as charming and resonating as ever.

Surya found himself lost in the same vivid flashback. It was as if he was standing at the school gate once again, watching Anshu with the same silent admiration he had always harboured. She was vibrant, surrounded by friends, her laughter ringing through the air. Her energy and kindness had always set her apart, making her the unspoken leader of their group. He had always been too shy to approach her, content to admire from afar.

Now, here she was, calling his name, bringing all those old memories rushing back.

"Anshu? Is that really you?" Surya asked, his voice tinged with disbelief.

"Yes, it's me! It's been so long. How are you? What are you up to these days? Where are you headed?" Anshu's words tumbled out in a rush; her excitement evident.

Surya laughed, feeling the warmth of their shared history wash over him. "I'm good! After 10th grade, I lost touch with everyone. I missed the reunion too. What about you? What have you been doing all these years?"

Anshu smiled, a touch of nostalgia in her eyes. "I'm doing well. I work at Wipro now as a senior developer."

"Surya where are you heading now," Surya enquired.

Anshu replied, "I'm on my way to Annavaram".

Anshu added, "Oh, I almost forgot to ask, where are you headed?"

"I'm also going to Annavaram. What a coincidence!" Surya said, his eyes lighting up.

"Are you following me?" Anshu teased, laughing.

"Maybe! Just kidding, I'm with a friend." He gestured to Aahana, who waved at Anshu with a friendly smile.

Anshu waved back. "Nice to meet you, Aahana."

Aahana smiled warmly. "Likewise!"

Again, they both came to the conversation after giving the introduction to each other.

"So, how's life after tenth." Surya enquired.

"After 10th grade, we moved to Hyderabad for my dad's business, and we settled there. How about you? What have you been up to?" Ahana replied.

"I'm in software, like everyone else. There's always some dissatisfaction in this field, but it pays the bills," Surya replied, a hint of resignation in his voice.

Anshu nodded understandingly. "Yeah, I understand. Life seems good for you, though."

"It's alright. There's always a sense of unfulfillment, but we manage. What about you? How have things been?" Surya asked, genuinely curious about her life.

Surya and Anshu continued talking, their conversation effortlessly drifting back to the days of their school years. Surya found it hard to believe that he was sitting across from his old crush, someone he had admired from afar for so long. As they spoke, he couldn't help but smile, marvelling at how life had brought them together again after all these years.

They reminisced about their tenth-grade days, recalling the laughter, the challenges, and the friendships that had defined that time. Anshu animatedly talked about their old classmates, sharing stories about their antics and the memorable moments they had created together. She spoke of how their friend group had navigated the ups and downs of school life, from the pressure of exams to the excitement of school events.

Surya listened intently, his admiration for Anshu growing with each passing minute. He found himself becoming an absorbed listener, hanging on to her every word. Anshu's enthusiasm was infectious, and her recollections brought back a flood of memories for Surya. He nodded along, adding his own memories to the mix, but mostly, he was content to let Anshu lead the conversation.

They talked about their favourite teachers, the ones who had inspired them and the ones who had made them groan with their strictness. Anshu laughed as she recalled the time their math teacher had given an impromptu quiz and how they had all struggled to solve the problems under his watchful eye. Surya smiled, remembering how Anshu had always managed to keep her composure, even in the most stressful situations.

"Remember Mr. Rao?" Anshu said, her eyes twinkling. "He was so strict, but he had a soft spot for our class."

Surya nodded, chuckling. "Yeah, he pretended to be tough, but he always let us get away with a lot more than he should have."

Anshu leaned forward, her voice lowering conspiratorially. "Do you remember that time he caught us passing notes during his lecture? He pretended to be furious but couldn't hide his smile."

Surya laughed. "Oh, absolutely! And the notes weren't even about the class. We were planning the school trip!"

The conversation shifted to their school activities and the various events they had participated in. Anshu spoke about the annual sports day, where she had cheered for her friends and participated in relay races. Surya remembered her energy and spirit, how she had always been the one to encourage others, no matter how tough the competition got.

"I was always in awe of your energy during those events," Surya confessed. "You were like the heart of the team."

Anshu shrugged modestly. "I just loved being part of the action. Remember how we used to practice for weeks before the sports day?"

Surya nodded. "Yeah, and you were always the one pushing us to do better. You had this way of making everyone believe we could win."

They also reminisced about their study sessions and the late-night preparations for exams. Anshu recalled how they had all gathered at a friend's house to study for their social studies exam, drinking endless cups of coffee to stay awake. Surya chuckled, recalling how Anshu had been the one to keep everyone focused, gently nudging them to get back to their books whenever they got distracted.

"Those study sessions were something else," Surya said, shaking his head with a smile. "I don't think we would've survived without your guidance."

Anshu laughed. "Well, someone had to keep you guys on track. But it was always a team effort. We all helped each other."

Throughout the conversation, Surya remained an attentive listener, soaking in every detail Anshu shared. He realized that he had always admired her not just for her looks, but for her kindness, her intelligence, and her unwavering support for those around her. Anshu had a way of making everyone feel important, and it was no different now.

As they talked, Surya found himself reflecting on how much had changed since those days, and yet, how some things remained the same. Anshu's positivity and warmth were still as strong as ever, and he felt a renewed sense of connection with her. It was as if no time had passed at all, and they were back in their school uniforms, navigating the challenges of their teenage years together.

The conversation flowed easily, moving from topic to topic, each memory bringing a new wave of nostalgia. Surya felt a sense of peace and contentment, grateful for this unexpected reunion with Anshu. It was a reminder of how life had a way of bringing people back together, of rekindling old connections and creating new memories.

"Do you remember the farewell party?" Anshu asked, her eyes sparkling with the memory. "We all dressed up and danced like there was no tomorrow."

Surya nodded, a smile spreading across his face. "How could I forget? That was the night I involved myself in the world. And by the way you looked stunning in that blue dress."

Anshu blushed slightly, smiling. "Thank you. It was such a magical night. We all felt so grown-up and ready to take on the world."

As the night wore on, Surya and Anshu continued to talk, their bond growing stronger with each shared memory. It was a moment of reflection and reconnection, a chance to relive the past and look forward to the future. And through it all, Surya remained an admired listener, captivated by the stories of the girl who had once been his crush and who now, once again, held a special place in his heart.

After some time, Anshu fell deep into thought, her gaze distant as she processed the flood of emotions and memories. Surya noticed her silence and gently nudged her.

"What are you thinking about?" he asked, his voice soft with concern.

Anshu smiled, her eyes meeting his. "Just wondering how many twists and turns life has. By the way, who is she?"

Surya glanced over at Aahana, who was engrossed in a book. "She's Aahana, my friend. I introduced before."

Anshu with doubt, "I am not asking about that, is there something running between you two".

Surya with no pause, "we met by accident and things happened and let us travel together and nothing more to it. She is a good friend".

Anshu understands what Surya want to convey.

Later Surya invited Aahana to join their conversation, and she moved over, her book still in hand.

"Nice to meet you, Aahana," Anshu said warmly.

"Likewise," Aahana replied, her smile genuine.

As the girls began to talk, Surya felt a bit out of place, the conversation quickly turning to topics he knew little about. He watched them for a moment before deciding to give them some space, pulling out a book of his own to read.

The train continued its journey, and they all chatted about their lives, work, and old memories. When the train arrived at the next station, Surya got off to buy water and snacks, returning with a few bottles and packets of chips.

"Thanks, Surya," Anshu said, taking a bottle from him.

"No problem. By the way, did your parents call you during the trip?" Surya asked, a hint of concern in his voice.

"Yes, they did. They know I'm not alone now," Anshu replied with a reassuring smile.

"That's good. I was just making sure," Surya said, feeling a sense of relief.

"Thanks for looking out for me," Anshu added, her gratitude evident.

Time passed, Ahana informed both Surya and Anshu. "I am going to sleep wake me when the station arrives".

Both of them nodded to Ahana, and resume the conversation about their school days.

As the conversation continued, Surya and Anshu became so engrossed in their memories that they lost track of time. The train chugged along, the rhythmic clatter of the wheels creating a soothing background to their animated exchange. Their laughter filled the compartment as they shared one story after another, diving deeper into the reservoir of their shared past.

Surya felt a sense of warmth and familiarity as Anshu recounted the tales of their school days. It was as if the years had melted away, leaving behind the essence of their youthful camaraderie. They spoke about their mutual friends, the silly pranks, the memorable school trips, and the crushes that had seemed so important back then. Every anecdote Anshu shared painted a vivid picture of their shared experiences, making Surya realize how much he had cherished those moments.

Anshu's eyes sparkled with excitement as she narrated the tale of their tenth-grade farewell party, where she had danced with her friends, creating a spectacle that had left everyone in stitches. Surya remembered standing on the sidelines, watching her with admiration. He smiled at the memory, realizing how much had changed since then.

Lost in the conversation, they didn't notice the hours slipping by. The train journey, which had initially seemed daunting, now felt like a brief interlude in their ongoing dialogue. They were so absorbed in their exchange that the world outside the train became a distant blur.

Suddenly, a faint announcement crackled over the train's PA system, breaking the spell of their conversation. "Next station, Annavaram."

The announcement brought a sense of reality back to their whimsical journey down memory lane. Both Anshu and Surya looked at each other, the realization that their time together on the train was nearing its end sinking in.

Surya smiled, a mixture of nostalgia and contentment in his eyes. "Looks like we're almost there."

"Yeah," Anshu replied, her voice tinged with wistfulness. "But I'm glad we had this time to catch up. It's been really nice."

Surya nodded. "It really has. It's amazing how life brings people back together in the most unexpected ways."

As the train began to slow down, preparing to arrive at the station, they both felt a sense of anticipation and a renewed sense of connection. They gathered their belongings, preparing to disembark.

Surya wakes Ahana and said we arrived at the destination.

Ahana wakes up and collect her belonging to get off the train.

The journey had been more than just a train ride; it had been a chance to relive cherished memories and rekindle an old friendship.

As they stepped off the train and into the bustling station, Anshu, Surya, and Ahana felt a sense of possibility. Their paths had crossed again, and who knew what the future held? For now, they were content to enjoy the moment, grateful for the twists and turns of life that had brought them back together.

Ahana, ever the enthusiastic friend, was the first to break the silence. "This place has changed so much!" she exclaimed, her eyes wide with wonder as she took in the busy platforms and the throngs of travellers rushing to their destinations.

Anshu nodded, a smile playing on her lips. "It really has. I remember this station being much quieter back in the day."

Surya watched Anshu as they walked, memories of watching her leave the school grounds flooding his mind. He had always felt a pang of sadness as she cycled away, wishing he had the courage to say something, anything. Today, though, he felt a sense of fulfilment. Life had given him another chance, and he was determined not to let it slip away.

Surya, walking slightly behind the two women, watched them with a warm smile. He felt a deep sense of contentment seeing Anshu and Ahana so animated and happy. It was as if no time had passed since their school days, and they were all back together, just like old times.

They made their way through the crowd, weaving between travellers and vendors. The sounds of the station—announcements over the loudspeaker, the chatter of passengers, the clinking of metal wheels—created a lively symphony that filled the air.

As they exited the station, Ahana turned to Surya and Anshu with a grin. "So, what's the plan now? I say we grab a coffee and catch up some more. What do you guys think?"

Anshu laughed. "Sounds perfect. There's a little café nearby that I used to love. Let's go there."

Surya nodded in agreement, his heart light. "Lead the way, Anshu."

Walking side by side, the three friends headed toward the café, their conversation flowing easily. They spoke of their current lives, sharing stories about their careers, families, and the paths that had led them back to this moment.

Surya asked Anshu for her reason to visit Annavaram.

Anshu replied, "yah, about that I forgot to mention I am getting married Surya"

After listening to the shocking news Ahana looks for Surya reaction.

Surya seems he never cares much about Anshu being married.

Anshu continues the story, "How her parents arranged the marriage alliance with the guy named Harsha, and how she finds comfort in meeting Harsha and the story after and how she ended up here."

Surya and Ahana sits there listening to the story narrated by Anshu.

As they settled into a cozy corner of the café, sipping on steaming cups of coffee, the sense of possibility that had filled the air at the station lingered. The future was uncertain, but it was also wide open, brimming with potential. For now, they were content to bask in the joy of their reunion, knowing that whatever came next, they would face it together.

CHAPTER XIII

Annavaram

After finishing their coffee, they decided to head to the temple. Stepping outside the café, they found a cab and set off.

"Shall we find a place to stay first?" Surya suggested, looking between the two women.

Anshu nodded, "Yes, let's find a room to freshen up before we head to the temple."

Ahana, always the practical one, agreed quickly. "I think that's a good idea. We can leave our bags and take a moment to rest."

Navigating through the bustling crowd, they made their way to a nearby lodge known for its proximity to the temple. The lodge was modest but clean, offering a warm welcome to the pilgrims and travellers who frequented it. The walk through the town, with its narrow, winding streets and the occasional burst of laughter or conversation, felt like a step back in time.

Surya approached the receptionist and asked for a room. "We need a room for the day, please."

The receptionist, an elderly man with kind eyes, glanced at the three of them and quickly assigned a room. "Room 203 is available. It has two beds and plenty of space. Will that work for you?"

Surya nodded, accepting the key. "That will be perfect, thank you."

They made their way to the room, and as they entered, Surya turned to Anshu and Ahana. "Let's freshen up and then we can head to the temple. It's best to visit in the early morning when it's cooler and less crowded."

Anshu and Ahana both agreed. They unpacked their bags and took turns freshening up. The room was simple but comfortable, with two beds and a small sitting area. The walls were adorned with traditional artwork, and the faint scent of sandalwood lingered in the air. As they prepared for their temple visit, the sense of camaraderie and shared purpose filled the room.

After a short rest, they gathered their things and set out for the temple. The sun was beginning to rise, casting a golden hue over Annavaram. The temple, perched on a hill, looked majestic against the morning sky. The path to the temple was lined with vendors selling flowers, incense, and small idols, each adding to the sacred ambiance of the place.

Walking together, Surya found himself caught between two important people in his life: Anshu, his old school crush who had unexpectedly re-entered his life, and Ahana, who had become a close and cherished friend. The blend of past and present made this journey even more significant. He marvelled at how life's paths twisted and turned, bringing unexpected reunions and newfound friendships.

As they climbed the steps to the temple, the sounds of the city below faded, replaced by the peaceful chants and the scent of incense. The steps were worn smooth by the countless devotees who had climbed them over the years, each step a testament to faith and devotion. They reached the top and stood before the temple, taking in its serene beauty.

The grandeur of the place took their breath away. The temple stood tall, its intricately carved gopuram illuminated by the soft glow of the evening lights. Devotees thronged the entrance, their faces lit with devotion and anticipation. The gopuram, with its intricate sculptures and vivid colours, told stories of gods and legends, each figure etched with meticulous care.

Surya looked at Anshu and Ahana, both of whom seemed moved by the experience. "I'm glad we're here together," he said softly.

Anshu smiled, her eyes reflecting the warmth of their shared memories. "Me too, Surya. It feels like everything has come full circle."

Ahana, ever the pragmatic one, nodded. "It's good to take a moment like this, to reflect and find peace."

They entered the temple, participating in the rituals and offering their prayers. The ambiance inside was tranquil, filled with the sounds of devotees chanting and the gentle ring of bells. Surya felt a deep sense of calm wash over him, as if the worries and uncertainties of the past were being gently lifted away. The inner sanctum, bathed in the flickering light of oil lamps, felt like a haven of peace.

After their prayers, they sat together on the temple steps, watching the sun dip below the horizon. The sky was painted with hues of orange and pink, creating a picturesque backdrop to their shared moment of peace. The view from the temple, overlooking the town and the surrounding countryside, was breathtaking.

Surya turned to Anshu and Ahana, feeling grateful for their presence. "Thank you for being here. This means a lot to me."

Anshu reached out and squeezed his hand. "We're here for you, Surya. Always."

Ahana smiled, her eyes reflecting the same sentiment. "Yes, always."

As they sat together, the ambience settling in around them, Surya felt a profound sense of connection and clarity. This journey to Annavaram had not only been a pilgrimage to a holy site but also a pilgrimage of the heart, bringing together the threads of his past and present in a tapestry of friendship and understanding. The peacefulness of the moment was a stark contrast to the chaos of their arrival, underscoring the tranquillity they had found.

Stepping out of the temple, they were enveloped in the cool evening air, filled with a serene calmness. Walking back to their lodge, their steps were unhurried and contemplative. The streetlights are still on and casting shadows, and the sounds of the town slowly becoming rowdy as the vendor setting their shops.

• • •

As they walked back, each step they took revealed more of Annavaram's charm. The streets were lined with traditional houses, their facades adorned with vibrant rangoli designs. The smell of jasmine flowers and incense wafted through the air, mingling with the distant sound of temple bells.

Surya observed the lively market stalls, now opening for the morning, with vendors placing out their goods. The colourful displays of spices, textiles, and handmade crafts spoke of a rich cultural heritage. He watched as a group of children ran past, their laughter echoing through the narrow alleyways, a reminder of the timelessness of joy.

Ahana, walking beside him, seemed deep in thought. She had always been the one to ground him, her practicality a steady anchor in their friendship. He wondered what she was reflecting on, as the golden lights of the streetlamps illuminated her thoughtful expression.

Anshu, on his other side, seemed lost in her own memories. The soft glow of the morning lights highlighted her features, making her look ethereal. Surya couldn't help but think back to their school days, the innocent crush he had on her, and how life had brought them back together in this moment.

Reaching the lodge, they entered their room and settled down. Surya took a moment to reflect on the day. The unexpected reunion with Anshu, the comfortable camaraderie with Ahana, and the serene beauty of the temple all combined to create a profound sense of peace within him.

Anshu broke the silence. "Surya, do you remember the last time we saw each other? It was at the Social exam."

Surya smiled, recalling the memory. "Yes, I do. It feels like a lifetime ago."

Ahana, curious, asked, "What was it like? Your school days?"

Surya and Anshu exchanged a glance, and she began to share stories from their school days. They talked late into the afternoon, their laughter and reminiscing creating a warm and intimate atmosphere.

Ahana, listening to their tales, felt a deeper connection forming. She realized that this journey was not just about visiting the temple but about understanding the layers of Surya's past, which made their friendship even more meaningful.

Eventually, they all settled down to eat their lunch. Then left for the nearest restaurant to eat.

While they are having their lunch Anshu brought the topic, "what's next, what are your plans."

"Nothing just go with the flow," Ahana answered.

"Oh ok, I need to catch my train in the night." Anshu informed.

Surya replied, "oh so you are leaving today."

"Yah, there are so many marriage works to be done." Anshu replied.

Both Ahana and Surya nodded their heads understandingly.

Then three of them completed their lunch and left to their room where Anshu insisted to take rest being restless last night.

Surya and Ahana nodded understandingly.

All three of them lay's down to have some rest. In the room filled with the soft sounds of their breathing. Surya lay awake for a while, thinking about how this trip had already changed him. The journey to Annavaram had begun as a simple pilgrimage but was turning into a transformative experience.

As he drifted off to sleep, Surya felt a profound sense of gratitude. Life's unexpected turns had brought him here, to this moment, with two important people by his side. The past, present, and future seemed to merge, creating a tapestry of memories, emotions, and newfound understanding.

In the evening, they woke up to the gentle light of evening filtering through the windows. Anshu stretched and smiled at Surya and Ahana. "Shall we explore more of Annavaram before I leave?"

Ahana nodded enthusiastically. "Yes, let's make the most of our time here."

Surya agreed, feeling a renewed sense of purpose. They set out together, ready to discover more of the town's beauty, history, and the bonds that tied them together.

• • •

The town of Annavaram welcomed them with its evening hustle and bustle. They wandered through the markets, admiring the local crafts and savouring the vibrant atmosphere.

As they explored, Surya couldn't help but feel a sense of wonder at how life had brought them all here. The journey was more than just a visit to a sacred site; it was a journey of the heart, bringing them closer to each other and to themselves.

The day's adventures further deepened their bond. They visited the temple again, this time in the diming evening light, and participated in the evening rituals. The sense of peace and spirituality was even profound in the evening.

They also visited nearby attractions, learning about the history and culture of Annavaram. Each place they visited, each story they heard, added another layer to their shared experience.

As the day drew to a close, they found themselves back at the temple steps, watching the sunset once again. The sky was a canvas of brilliant colours, reflecting the beauty of their journey together

• • •

Surya turned to Anshu and Ahana, feeling a deep sense of contentment. "This has been an incredible journey. Thank you for being a part of it."

Anshu smiled; her eyes filled with warmth. "Thank you for bringing us here, Surya. This has been a journey of discovery for all of us."

Ahana nodded, her expression thoughtful. "Yes, a journey of the heart."

As they sat together, watching the sunset, they felt a profound sense of connection and peace.

The evening air was cool, and the atmosphere around the temple was filled with a serene calmness.

As like that time passes by them sitting and chitchatting on the steps of Annavaram.

Night falls on them, Anshu reminded about the train she has to catch.

All three of them started to their room.

After reaching room, Anshu left for freshening up.

Surya stayed outside in the balcony and arranging all his taught about the day they have spent till then.

Ahana is watching Surya from the room. Came outside to Surya and asked, "what is it Surya, have you decided to confess your feelings".

"What are you saying" Surya puzzled.

"I know she is the one you have crush on I remember you mentioning her" Ahana gives a firm reply.

Surya with a pause, "yes, it is true but it is long back in my school days that has nothing to do with me now. And more importantly she getting married soon."

Ahana answered puzzled Surya, "Surya, the movement you saw her I find it in your eyes that you have never forgotten her. So, what is wrong in letting her know your feelings."

Surya still puzzled, "she has her own life to care why should I burden her with mine."

Ahana after a gap, she took a deep breath. "Surya, let me confess about something. This trip to Annavaram is planned by me to let you meet Anshu and get your closure and move on."

Surya was stunned. "You planned all this?"

Ahana nodded. "I knew that what you felt back then wasn't just infatuation. It wasn't just a teenage crush. You haven't had those feelings for anyone else since her. That told me that you never moved on from her. I thought you should know that. And since time waits for no one, I had to act now. Live in the moment, Surya. Go and speak your heart out to her."

Surya, still in shock, agreed. "Alright, I'll go talk to her."

Surya said to Anshu that "Ahana is asleep".

Later Anshu and Surya started to railway station.

After reaching the railway station. They both sat on the platform waiting for the train.

Anshu looked at him, sensing something was off. "Okay. You know, my wedding is fixed. I have the invitation card with me. I wanted to give it to you earlier, but I thought I'd give it to you now instead."

She handed him the card. Surya looked at it, his heart sinking. "What do you do now?" he asked, trying to make small talk.

"I'm a senior developer," Anshu replied. "By the way, my train hasn't arrived yet. We still have time."

Surya nodded, the weight of what he needed to say pressing down on him. "Anshu, there's something I've been wanting to tell you for the past nine years. I've struggled with these feelings, and I know this might not be the right time or place, but I need to say this."

Anshu listened silently; her eyes focused on him.

"Ever since you left school, I've never moved on from you. I know it sounds immature, but I never stopped admiring you. Loving someone isn't something you learn; it's something you feel. And I felt that for you. I didn't try to stop you from leaving back then, and maybe that was my mistake. It took me a long time to understand what loving someone really means. Knowing that you're getting married and saying all this feels awkward. I thought I could keep these feelings to myself, but Ahana made me realize that I need to tell you. Not for your sake, but for mine. You were my first crush, Anshu. And even though I never expressed it, I always admired you. I needed you to know this because, without telling you, it feels like my feelings never existed."

Anshu was silent, absorbing his words. She then took a deep breath and replied, "I knew you liked me back then, and I know it now. But I never felt the same way about you. I didn't want to give you false hope, so I kept my distance. I'm glad you told me this now, Surya. It's good that you finally let it out. But my feelings haven't changed. I never had those feelings for you, and I still don't. But I'm happy you shared this with me. It means you can finally move on."

Surya after listening to Anshu and letting her know his feelings make his heart lighter and he even feels a lot of burden is put down from him.

As Surya experiencing something new in his life. The train that Anshu has to take have entered the railway station.

Surya with a relief in heart starts smiling wholeheartedly. "I hope you find all the happiness you deserve, Anshu. Thank you for listening."

Anshu nodded, extending her hand. "Take care, Surya. And thank you for being honest with me."

Surya shook her hand. "You too, Anshu. Goodbye."

He watched as she boarded her train, feeling a mix of relief and sorrow. He had finally said what he needed to, even if it didn't change anything.

Surya while watching Anshu from the window, "Anshu, before you go, there's a photo I want to share with you. It's something that's been with me for a long time."

Anshu replied "Sure, I'll look at it."

Surya opened his phone, "I have sent you through WhatsApp. By the way this is not something I want you to react. But according to me this is something which rightfully belongs to you while I am carrying from so long."

Anshu after watching the message pop-up, "Thank you, Surya. Take care, and we'll stay in touch."

Surya with smile on the face, "Take care, Anshu. Safe travels."

As Anshu boarded the train, Surya stood there, feeling a sense of closure and readiness to embrace whatever the future held for him.

Train started moving and then final waves between Surya and Anshu takes place. And the Anshu goes through her phone and finds that Surya has sent her a pic which seems like a letter he wrote.

She just starts reading the letter.

***

A Letter from Surya to Anshu

Hi Anshu,

I never thought I'd write a letter in my life, but here I am writing my heart out.

You are the reason why I write this letter.

And you are the inspiration behind what I write in this letter.

I may have never told you how much I like you, and you might not even be aware of it, but my love for you is real. Loving you makes me happy, and that's the reason which makes me feel human.

Many people come and go in our lives, but only a few introduce us to love. You are that person in my life, and your charm is beyond compare. In a world where people tend to break-up/divorce for any reason, you gave me a reason to fall in love and a reason to believe in it.

I can't explain why, where, or how this love for you blossomed, but the feeling of loving you made me realize something profound. The love I feel is not just because of you; it's because of what you bring out in me. This love, no matter where I am or what I'm doing, will always stay with me because it was born from you.

With love,

Surya.

****

"As Surya poured out his heart in this letter, Anshu felt overwhelmed. She listened to his words out directly from the letter, understanding the depth of his emotions. She realized that no reply could truly encapsulate or reciprocate the feelings Surya had held onto for so long. Anshu knew that anything she said would fall short of acknowledging the weight of his emotions and the significance of this moment for him. She respected his courage and felt a profound sense of gratitude for his honesty, even as she struggled to find the right words to respond.

Anshu just cherished Surya's letter by watching the scenery from the window.

Then Surya returned to the lodge, where Ahana was waiting.

"How did it go?" she asked.

"I told her everything. She listened, but she doesn't feel the same way. But it's okay. I feel lighter now," Surya replied.

Ahana smiled. "Good. Now, let's move forward. The future has a lot in store for you, Surya."

Surya nodded, feeling a newfound sense of freedom. It was time to look ahead and embrace whatever came next."

***

"*Surya, That night with his newfound freedom slept like a baby.*"

CHAPTER XIV

The Unexpected Journey

Surya awoke to the soft, insistent prodding of Ahana. The morning sun gently crept into the room, casting a warm glow on Surya's face. He stirred and slowly opened his eyes, feeling an unexpected sense of lightness and peace after his heartfelt conversation with Anshu the previous night. As he blinked awake, he saw Ahana standing by the window, already energized and eager to start the day. Her silhouette was outlined by the sun's rays, creating a halo-like effect around her.

"Wake up, sleepyhead! There's so much to do today," Ahana said with a bright smile, her eyes sparkling with excitement. "I have a whole itinerary planned, from Annavaram to Vizag. We're going to visit so many places: the INS Kurusura Submarine Museum, the Varaha Lakshmi Narasimha Temple, Borra Caves, the Biodiversity Park, Kailasagiri, Araku Valley, Rishikonda Beach, Rama Krishna Beach, and more."

Surya stretched and yawned, feeling unusually refreshed. He propped himself up on his elbows, taking in the sight of Ahana, who was practically bouncing with anticipation. Her enthusiasm was infectious, and he felt a surge of energy.

"Alright, alright. I'm up. What's the plan?" he asked, rubbing the sleep from his eyes.

Ahana's grin widened. "It's going to be an adventure!" she exclaimed, clapping her hands together. Her excitement was palpable, and Surya couldn't help but smile.

Surya quickly realized that he had only packed for a short trip, with just two pairs of clothes and a small bag. "Ahana, if we're going to Vizag, we'll need more clothes and a bigger bag to carry everything. I think we should also book a car for rental. What do you say?"

Ahana nodded, her eyes twinkling with agreement. "You're right. Let's get ready and head out. We have a lot to do!"

They both prepared to leave for Vizag, packing their belongings and checking out of the hotel. The anticipation of the upcoming journey made even the mundane tasks exciting. As they headed towards the bus station, the hustle and bustle of the early morning crowd added to the sense of adventure.

The bus ride to Vizag was filled with anticipation. The scenery transformed from urban landscapes to lush greenery and scenic vistas as they approached the coastal city. Ahana chatted excitedly about their plans, her energy contagious. Surya found himself smiling more than he had in a long time, feeling the weight of his past lifting.

Upon arriving in Vizag, they headed straight to a nearby mall. The mall was bustling with people, the air filled with the scent of freshly brewed coffee and the sound of laughter. Surya picked out some casual clothes and a sturdy backpack to carry their essentials for the trip. Ahana helped him choose, offering fashion advice with a playful glint in her eye.

"You need to look good for our adventure," she teased, holding up a bright blue shirt. "How about this one?"

Surya chuckled, taking the shirt from her. "I think it suits me," he said, trying it on and striking a pose. Ahana laughed, and for a moment, everything felt light and carefree.

Once they were equipped with their new gear, they made their way to a car rental service. They chose a comfortable vehicle that would make their journey around the city and its surrounding areas more convenient. The car was a sleek, silver sedan that promised a smooth ride. Surya adjusted the rearview mirror, glancing at Ahana who was busy checking the map.

"Ready for our first stop?" he asked, starting the engine.

"Absolutely!" Ahana replied, buckling her seatbelt with a determined look. "Let's go!"

• • •

Day 1: Vizag Adventures

Their first stop was the INS Kurusura Submarine Museum. Standing on the sandy shores of RK Beach, the decommissioned submarine turned museum was an impressive sight. The massive steel structure loomed over them, a testament to naval engineering and history. As they walked through the tight, metal corridors, the echoes of their footsteps filled the silence. The museum was a maze of narrow passageways, filled with dials, levers, and gauges that spoke of a bygone era.

"This is incredible," Surya said, marvelling at the machinery. "Imagine living in these cramped quarters for months on end."

Ahana nodded, her eyes wide with awe. "It's like stepping into a different world. The bravery and dedication of the sailors are truly inspiring."

The museum provided a unique glimpse into life underwater, and they left with a newfound respect for naval officers. The experience was both humbling and fascinating, leaving them deep in thought as they made their way to their next destination.

Next, they visited the Varaha Lakshmi Narasimha Temple. The ancient temple, perched atop Simhachalam Hill, was a spiritual experience. The climb up the hill was steep, but the reward was worth it. The temple's intricate carvings and serene atmosphere left them in awe. As they entered the sanctum, the scent of incense and the sound of chanting filled the air.

Ahana offered her prayers, her eyes closed in deep concentration. Surya took a moment to reflect, finding a sense of peace in the sacred surroundings. The temple's architecture was stunning, with every pillar and wall telling a story of devotion and craftsmanship.

After a spiritually enriching morning, they headed to a nearby restaurant for lunch, savouring traditional Andhra cuisine. The flavours were a delightful mix of spicy and tangy, each dish a culinary masterpiece. Ahana's eyes lit up as she tasted the gongura pachadi, a local specialty.

"This is amazing, Surya! You've got to try this," she said, offering him a spoonful.

Surya tasted it and nodded in agreement. "It's delicious. I think we should definitely explore more local food while we're here."

With their appetites satisfied, they set off for Kailasagiri. They took a cable car ride to the top of the hill, enjoying panoramic views of the city and the coastline. The ride was exhilarating, with the ground dropping away beneath them and the city unfolding below. The park atop the hill offered numerous attractions, including statues of Shiva and Parvati, beautifully landscaped gardens, and an impressive viewpoint that provided a breathtaking vista of the Bay of Bengal.

"This view is incredible," Surya said, his eyes scanning the horizon. "It's like we're on top of the world."

Their final stop for the day was the Biodiversity Park - Botanical Garden. The lush greenery and diverse flora provided a refreshing change of pace. They strolled through the garden, taking in the vibrant colours and the fragrant scents of the various plants. The garden was a haven of tranquillity, with the gentle rustling of leaves and the chirping of birds creating a soothing backdrop.

"This place is beautiful," Ahana said, her voice filled with wonder. "It's like a little piece of paradise."

Surya agreed, feeling the stress of the past few days melt away. "I could spend hours here."

As the sun began to set, they made their way back to their hotel, feeling content and fulfilled. The day's adventures had brought them closer and filled them with a sense of wonder and appreciation for the beauty of the world around them.

• • •

Day 2: Exploring the Hills and Beaches

On the second day we wake up in the early morning and started to our next journey to the Borra Caves. The drive to the caves took them through winding roads, surrounded by lush greenery and rolling hills. The limestone caves, with their stunning stalactites and stalagmites, were a natural wonder. As they ventured deeper into the caves, the cool, damp air and the play of light and shadows created an otherworldly atmosphere.

"This is like something out of a fantasy novel," Ahana whispered, her voice echoing off the cave walls.

Surya nodded, equally mesmerized. "It's amazing how nature can create such beauty."

The guided tour provided fascinating insights into the history and formation of the caves. They learned about the local legends associated with the caves, adding a mystical element to the experience.

Ahana smiled, her face glowing with excitement. "I could stay up here forever."

After spending a few hours exploring the Borra caves, they drove to Araku Valley. The journey to the valley was a picturesque one, with winding roads that offered stunning views of the surrounding hills and forests. The valley, with its rolling hills and coffee plantations, was a nature lover's paradise. They visited the tribal museum, learning about the indigenous tribes and their unique culture.

The museum was a treasure trove of artifacts, each piece telling a story of a rich and vibrant heritage. Ahana was particularly fascinated by the traditional jewellery and clothing, while Surya found the musical instruments intriguing.

The highlight of the visit was the Araku Coffee House, where they savoured freshly brewed coffee made from locally grown beans. The rich, aromatic coffee was a treat for the senses, and they spent a leisurely hour sipping their drinks and enjoying the serene surroundings.

"This is the best coffee I've ever had," Ahana declared, taking a sip. "We should take some beans home."

Surya agreed, buying a few bags as souvenirs. "Absolutely. This is too good to leave behind."

After getting tired from exploring the beauty of Araku, Surya and Ahana feels exhausted so they have to skip some places on the second day to take rest.

They just find the nearest hotel in Araku, and went there to rest themselves.

● ● ●

Day 3: Final Adventures

After the second day rest, they both woke up with good energy and started to Vizag to explore other iconic places in Vizag.

Returning to Vizag, they spent the afternoon at Rishikonda Beach. The pristine beach, with its golden sands and turquoise waters, was perfect for relaxation. Ahana and Surya enjoyed a leisurely walk along the shore, the gentle waves lapping at their feet. The beach was relatively quiet, with only a few other visitors scattered along the shore.

"This is perfect," Ahana said, her voice soft and content. "Just what we needed."

Surya nodded, feeling a deep sense of peace. "I couldn't agree more."

After that they visited to Rama Krishna Beach. The bustling beach was a hub of activity, with vendors selling snacks, souvenirs, and trinkets. The air was filled with the scent of street food and the sound of laughter and chatter. They walked along the sandy shores, dipping their toes in the water and watching the waves crash against the shore.

Ahana spotted a vendor selling local street food and tugged at Surya's arm. "Come on, let's try some!"

They indulged in local street food, relishing the flavours of Vizag. The spicy, tangy dishes were a delight, and they ate with gusto, laughing and chatting as they sampled different treats.

They watched the sunset, the sky ablaze with hues of orange and pink, creating a magical moment. The beauty of the scene was almost surreal, and they stood in silence, taking it all in.

As the sun set on their last day in Vizag, Surya and Ahana sat on the beach, reflecting on their journey. They had visited incredible places, created unforgettable memories, and grown closer as friends. Surya felt a deep sense of gratitude for Ahana's companionship and the experiences they had shared.

"Thank you, Ahana," he said softly, his voice filled with emotion.

She turned to him, surprised. "For what?"

"For everything. For making me live in the moment, for this incredible journey, and for being you."

Ahana smiled, her eyes twinkling with a mix of surprise and happiness. "I'm glad you're here with me, Surya. Let's make the most of every moment."

Surya nodded, feeling a sense of peace he hadn't felt in a long time. As they drove back to their hotel, he knew that this trip was just the beginning of many more adventures to come. They had explored new places, experienced new things, and most importantly, they had discovered new aspects of themselves and their friendship. The future was uncertain, but with Ahana by his side, Surya felt ready to face whatever it held.

✳✳✳

"*Their journey had been unexpected, but it had brought them closer and given them memories that would last a lifetime. Surya felt a sense of contentment. He was grateful for the journey, for the experiences, and for Ahana. He knew that, no matter what, they would always have this incredible adventure to look back on.*"

CHAPTER XV

The Surya no one Know's

Later that day Surya and Ahana arrived back at their hotel room, the air filled with a sense of both fulfilment and melancholy. The room, once a mere resting place, now felt like a repository of countless memories. They meticulously folded their clothes and zipped up their suitcases, each movement deliberate and unhurried. It wasn't just luggage they were packing; they were sealing away the laughter, exploration, and moments that had become precious treasures.

As Surya placed a neatly folded shirt into his suitcase, he paused, his fingers lingering on the fabric. The shirt was a vivid reminder of their visit to the Borra Caves, where the natural beauty had left them both in awe. He could almost feel the cool, damp air of the caves and hear Ahana's excited whispers echoing through the caverns. These memories seemed to hold a special place in their hearts, symbolizing the bond they had forged during this unforgettable journey.

After ensuring everything was in order, they returned the rental car, exchanging smiles with the friendly attendant who had helped them earlier. They headed to the railway station, the rhythmic clatter of their suitcases against the pavement harmonizing with the sounds of the bustling station. Their journey back to Hyderabad was filled with silent reflections, both of them lost in thoughts about the trip and what lay ahead. The train's gentle sway seemed to cradle their memories, lulling them into a state of contemplation.

Upon arriving in Hyderabad, Surya hailed a taxi to drop Ahana at her house. The drive was quiet, both of them immersed in their own worlds, yet connected by the shared silence. They exchanged warm goodbyes, their smiles tinged with the bittersweet reality of parting ways. As Surya watched Ahana disappear into her house, he felt a tug at his heart, a reminder of the deep connection they had formed.

When Surya reached his house, he knocked on the door, feeling a sense of anticipation mingled with nervousness. Swecha answered, and the instant she saw the smile on his face, her eyes lit up with joy. It had been a long time since she had seen him so genuinely happy. Surya greeted her warmly, enveloping her in a hug that spoke volumes about his transformed state of mind.

Surya then moved inside as he saw the family is all in the living room, he just turns to greet his uncle and aunt, who were equally shocked by his changed demeanour. This wasn't the Surya they knew – the introverted, reserved boy from childhood who often kept to himself. He exchanged pleasantries with them, his eyes sparkling with newfound vitality, and then excused himself to freshen up.

Everyone in the house was abuzz with curiosity, discussing the remarkable change in Surya's behaviour. His aunt, who had always been a keen observer, noted the subtle changes in his mannerisms. He seemed more at ease, more confident. After his bath, Surya joined his family in the living room, sitting beside his uncle on the sofa and watching TV. The familiarity of the setting brought back memories of simpler times.

His uncle, deeply moved, recalled the last time Surya had sat with them like this – back when he was in the sixth or seventh grade. He remembered a young boy, shy and introverted, who preferred the company of books over people. The transformation was astonishing, and unnoticed by Surya, tears welled up in his uncle's eyes, which his aunt and Swecha observed quietly.

Curiosity finally got the better of his uncle, who asked, "How was the trip, Surya?"

Surya replied, "It was good. Everything happened unexpectedly, and the thrill of the unknown made it even more exciting."

"So, who did you go with?" his uncle inquired, his curiosity piqued.

With a pause, Surya began to narrate the tale of his fall at the office, which led to a minor sprain. His family, unaware of this incident, listened intently. Surya didn't stop there. He talked about the girl whose medical file he had accidentally encountered, leading to his meeting with someone he now admired deeply.

As Surya narrated the story of Ahana, who was battling osteosarcoma, his family listened with rapt attention. They realized that this was not just a tale of a girl fighting cancer; it was the story of Surya discovering himself. He spoke about their trip to Annavaram and Vizag, detailing the places they explored, the people they met, and even the minutiae of their meals and accommodations.

He described the intricate carvings of the Varaha Lakshmi Narasimha Temple, the awe-inspiring stalactites and stalagmites of the Borra Caves, the serene beauty of Rishikonda Beach, and the bustling vibrancy of Rama Krishna Beach. Each place held a special memory, a moment of connection and discovery. Time seemed to stand still as Surya poured his heart out, sharing every detail about Ahana and their journey. His family, captivated by the story, felt a mix of emotions – joy for the changes in Surya and sadness for Ahana's condition. After the story ended, they went about their usual routines, processing everything they had heard.

Later, Surya's uncle invited him for a coffee at a nearby shop.

They both left to the coffee shop. There Surya goes through the menu in the coffee shop, in the mean time Surya asked his uncle, "what do you like to have uncle."

His uncle with not much consideration, "something regular will suffice".

As his uncle said Surya reached out to the employee there and ordered a filter coffee.

As they sipped their filter coffee, the familiar aroma mingling with the chatter of the shop, his uncle broached a sensitive topic. "Surya, what are you going to do now?" he asked, his tone gentle yet probing.

"About what, uncle?" Surya responded, slightly puzzled.

"I can see you're quite attached to Ahana, but she's not going to be with you for long. What will you do after...?" His uncle trailed off, seeing the blank look on Surya's face.

"Surya, this is the problem. You know what's going to happen, but you're not ready to accept it. Why?" his uncle pressed gently, his eyes searching Surya's for understanding.

"Surya, more than me you know yourself better. After your parent's left us, I saw you go through so much, which left you to be someone cooped all by yourself. I don't want that to be happening again" his uncle with concern.

Surya's mood shifted instantly. The brighter version of himself vanished, replaced by the introspective, troubled Surya his family was more familiar with. His uncle tried to lighten the mood, offering words of comfort and wisdom, but nothing seemed to work. They returned home, and

Surya retreated to his room, lost in thought.

Swecha, concerned, approached her father to understand what had happened. After learning about the conversation, she accepted it, knowing Surya needed to face these realities eventually. Life returned to its usual rhythm, with Surya going to the office and hospital each day, though his behaviour remained markedly different.

Phani, noticing Surya's troubled demeanour, asked about the trip. Surya, too preoccupied with his thoughts, barely acknowledged him. Lost in a whirlwind of emotions, Surya questioned whether he could bear losing Ahana. The thought of her absence turned his world upside down. Every moment with her seemed to be a precious countdown, and the impending loss loomed over him like a dark cloud.

Then Surya closed his eyes to rearrange his thoughts, so that he can do his work in peace.

When his eyes closed, Surya has figured Ahana face without much reasoning needed. Surya only remembers Ahana face with smile, nothing other than that he then makes a firm decision to see through his fears. He need see that smiley face again and again.

Eventually, Surya reminded himself that he needed to live in the present. He couldn't change the future or dwell on the past. Resolute, he decided to visit Ahana at the hospital. When he arrived, she was already there, waiting for him with ice cream in hand.

"Take your ice cream," Ahana said with a smile, her eyes twinkling with playful mischief.

"I thought you left," Surya replied, relief washing over him like a soothing balm.

"I had a gut feeling you'd be here, even if there was a tsunami in Hyderabad," she joked, her laughter light and infectious.

They shared a light moment, and Surya felt his worries fade into the background. He dropped Ahana home and returned to his office, apologizing to Phani for his earlier behaviour. The two shared a meaningful conversation, strengthening their bond and reminding Surya of the importance of friendship and support.

At home, Swecha noticed Surya's smile and felt reassured. His routine continued – work, hospital visits, and home – but with a newfound contentment. Days passed, and Surya's visits to the hospital became a cherished part of his day. Each visit was a reminder of the joy and strength Ahana brought into his life, despite her own struggles.

......

One day at the coffee shop, Ahana brought up the idea of another trip. "Surya, I'm thinking of going to Kerala. What do you think?" she asked excitedly, her eyes sparkling with anticipation.

Surya, taken aback by her sudden suggestion, leaned back in his chair, pondering the idea. "Kerala, huh? Sounds intriguing. What made you think of Kerala?"

Ahana's face lit up with enthusiasm. "I've always wanted to see the backwaters, the houseboats, and the lush greenery. Plus, I've heard the culture and food there are amazing!"

Surya smiled; her excitement contagious. "Alright, let's go. When should we book the tickets?"

Ahana clapped her hands in excitement. "How about next weekend? We can take a few days off and make the most of it."

Surya's mind raced with possibilities. "Can we take a flight?" he suggested, his excitement growing.

Ahana hesitated, practical considerations kicking in. "Flights are a bit costly."

Surya shrugged, his eyes twinkling with mischief. "I'm okay with it. I'm loaded, for God's sake."

Ahana laughed, her laughter ringing out in the coffee shop. "Okay, if I get a free ride."

Surya's grin widened. "Deal. Let's book the tickets."

They spent the next hour planning their trip, discussing the places they wanted to visit and the experiences they hoped to have. The idea of another adventure filled them both with anticipation and joy. Surya dropped Ahana home, their spirits high with the promise of a new journey.

Back at his place, Surya reflected on how quickly everything had happened. The idea of another trip filled him with hope and joy, and he couldn't wait to embark on this new journey with Ahana.

The next morning at 6:30 AM, Surya received a call from Ahana's number. Groggily, he answered, expecting a playful request to sneak out. Instead, he heard sobs and cries on the other end. Jolted awake, he demanded, "Who is this? What happened to Ahana?"

Ahana's mother, through her tears, delivered the devastating news: "Ahana is no more, Surya."

CHAPTER XVI

The Journey of Loss and Acceptance

The realization of Ahana's absence hit Surya like a wave, but strangely, he felt nothing. His mind was blank, devoid of any coherent thought or emotion. He got out of bed mechanically, as if his body was moving on autopilot, and walked to the main door. For a moment, it seemed like he was heading to Ahana's house, but instead, he just stepped outside and sat on the steps, staring into the void. The early morning air was cool, carrying with it the faint scent of jasmine from his aunt's garden.

His aunt, who was up early to start her day, noticed the open door. Concerned, she walked over and found Surya sitting there, the first light of dawn casting a pale glow on his face. She noticed the hollow look in his eyes and the way his shoulders slumped as if the weight of the world rested upon them.

"Surya, why are you awake so early? What are you doing here?" she asked gently, her voice filled with concern and confusion.

Surya remained silent, his gaze unfocused and distant. His aunt approached him and shook him lightly, trying to bring him back to reality. Her hands felt warm and comforting on his cold, rigid shoulders.

"Surya, what happened?" she asked again, her voice trembling slightly.

Surya finally responded, his voice devoid of emotion, flat and lifeless. "Ahana is no more, Aunt."

His aunt's face fell with sorrow, her eyes welling up with tears. She had known Ahana and had seen how much she meant to Surya. "What are you doing then? You need to go to her house for the last rites," she urged softly, trying to instil some sense of urgency.

Surya shook his head slowly. "I'm not going anywhere. I knew this was going to happen. I was prepared for it. Life goes on, and nothing is permanent. I think I need to go back to sleep. I have my night shift to attend," he said, getting up and heading back to his room, his steps heavy and unsteady. He locked the door behind him, shutting out the world and his own pain.

His aunt, distressed and unsure of what to do, woke Swecha and their uncle and informed them about Ahana. They all gathered outside Surya's door, but when his uncle knocked, there was no response.

"Let him be, Father," Swecha said softly, her voice laced with sorrow. "He needs to cope with this on his own."

Surya in the evening get's out of the room and just left to office. While the entire family is out looking for Surya to talk. But it doesn't take much time for them to understand today is not that day he talks.

Days turned into weeks as Surya went through the motions of his routine like an automaton. He woke up, got ready, went to the office, and came back home. He didn't speak to anyone, not even at work. His family was always there, waiting for him to open up, but he remained silent, his eyes vacant and his spirit broken.

• • •

Finally, one day, Swecha couldn't take it anymore. She confronted Surya as he was about to leave for work. The house was silent except for the ticking of the old grandfather clock in the hallway.

"What are you actually doing, Surya?" she demanded, her voice breaking the stillness of the morning.

Surya ignored her and tried to leave, but she grabbed his arm, her grip firm and unyielding. "Stop ignoring me and answer!"

Surya turned to her, his expression blank. "What is your problem? Is there something you want from me?" His tone was devoid of any warmth or recognition.

"Yes," Swecha said, her voice trembling with emotion. "I want the Surya I know. The one who, even if he didn't show it, cared for everyone around him. The Surya who noticed everything and cared in his own quiet way. I need you to be that Surya again."

Surya looked at her, confused and slightly irritated. "This is who I am. I've always been like this."

"No, you're not," Swecha insisted, her eyes pleading with him to understand. "You used to be aware of everything, even if you didn't show it. You cared, even if it was subconsciously. But now, you're shutting everyone out including your own pain. You need to accept what's happened and move on. Please, do something to bring the old Surya back."

Surya didn't respond. He left for work, but Swecha's words echoed in his mind, stirring something deep within him that he had buried. At the office, he found himself lost in thought, the usual hum of the office fading into the background.

Then out of nowhere, He remembered that he had bought tickets to Kerala for a trip he and Ahana had planned. The memory was bittersweet, tinged with the ache of loss and the warmth of her smile.

Impulsively, he sent a message to his family, informing them that he was going on a trip. Without any preparation, he went to the airport and started his journey to Kerala, the place that held so many dreams and memories.

Landing in Kerala, Surya was overwhelmed by a tumultuous mix of emotions. The beauty of the state, known as "God's Own Country," contrasted starkly with the emptiness he felt inside. He remembered Ahana's excitement about visiting Kochi, Alappuzha, Munnar, and other iconic places. Each location held a special significance for her, and he had promised to take her to all of them. Now, as he set out to visit these places alone, he couldn't shake the feeling that she was still with him, her presence as palpable as the humid air.

Surya's first stop was Kochi, a vibrant city with a rich colonial history. The streets were lined with Dutch and Portuguese architecture, each building telling a story of a bygone era. As he walked along the Fort Kochi beach, he remembered Ahana's fascination with the Chinese fishing nets. She had always wanted to see them up close. Surya stood there, watching the fishermen at work, feeling her excitement bubbling within him. He wandered through the narrow streets lined with quaint cafes and art galleries, imagining Ahana's delight at the vibrant art and culture that infused the city. At Mattancherry Palace, he felt her awe at the intricate murals depicting scenes from the Ramayana and Mahabharata. Kochi was a blend of old-world charm and modernity, much like Ahana herself.

From Kochi, Surya travelled to Alappuzha, known for its serene backwaters. Boarding a traditional houseboat, he could almost hear Ahana's laughter as they would have navigated the tranquil waters together. The lush green paddy fields and swaying coconut palms mirrored the serenity he craved. As the boat glided through the network of canals, he felt a sense of peace wash over him, as if

Ahana was there, soothing his troubled heart. The evening sunset, casting a golden glow over the waters, was a moment of profound beauty that he wished he could share with her.

Next, Surya headed to Munnar, a hill station renowned for its tea gardens and misty mountains. The winding roads leading up to Munnar were surrounded by sprawling tea plantations, the air heavy with the scent of fresh tea leaves. Surya recalled how Ahana had been eager to visit the Tata Tea Museum. Standing amidst the rolling hills, he felt her joy as if she were there, admiring the lush green landscape. The visit to the Eravikulam National Park, home to the endangered Nilgiri Tahr, was bittersweet. He could almost hear Ahana's voice, marvelling at the sight of the majestic creatures. The cool breeze and the panoramic views from Top Station felt like Ahana's gentle touch, reminding him of the shared dream they once had.

Surya's journey continued to Thekkady, known for the Periyar Wildlife Sanctuary. The boat ride on Periyar Lake, surrounded by dense forests, was a moment of introspection. He felt Ahana's adventurous spirit urging him to explore the wilderness. The sight of elephants, wild boars, and various birds filled him with a sense of wonder. He remembered Ahana's love for nature and how she would have been thrilled by the experience. Trekking through the forest, he felt a connection to her, as if she were guiding him through the dense foliage.

In Varkala, Surya found solace on the beach with its unique cliffs. The view of the Arabian Sea from the cliff was breathtaking. Surya sat there, the sound of the waves crashing against the rocks mingling with his thoughts. Ahana had always wanted to visit the Papanasam beach, known for its natural spring believed to have medicinal properties. Surya felt her presence as he walked along the beach, the cool water washing over his feet. The Janardhana Swamy Temple, perched on a cliff, was a place of spiritual significance, and Surya prayed for Ahana's peace, feeling her gratitude in his heart.

Wayanad, with its lush greenery and historical significance, was Surya's next destination. He visited the Edakkal Caves, where ancient petroglyphs spoke of a bygone era. Ahana had been fascinated by history, and Surya felt her excitement as he explored the caves. The visit to the Banasura Sagar Dam, the largest earthen dam in India, was awe-inspiring. Surya imagined Ahana's amazement at the vast expanse of water surrounded by hills. Trekking to the Meenmutty Falls, he felt her adventurous spirit pushing him forward, the cascading water reminding him of her free-spirited nature.

Surya's journey led him to Kumarakom, another backwater haven. The bird sanctuary here was a place Ahana had wanted to visit. Surya watched the myriad of birds, feeling Ahana's presence in the fluttering wings and melodious calls. The houseboat cruise on Vembanad Lake was a serene experience, the gentle rocking of the boat lulling him into a state of tranquillity. Surya felt a sense of closure, as if Ahana was with him, enjoying the beauty of the moment.

His next stop was Kovalam, a beach town known for its pristine beaches and vibrant culture. The Lighthouse Beach, with its iconic red and white striped lighthouse, was a place Ahana had dreamed of visiting. Surya climbed to the top of the lighthouse, the panoramic view of the coastline stretching before him. He felt a sense of fulfilment, as if he had carried Ahana's dreams with him and lived them for her. The sunset at Kovalam beach, with the sky painted in hues of orange and pink, was a moment of poignant beauty, a fitting end to his journey.

Finally, Surya visited Thiruvananthapuram, the capital city of Kerala. The Padmanabhaswamy Temple, known for its architectural beauty, was a place of deep spiritual significance. Surya felt Aahana's reverence as he walked through the temple complex. The Napier Museum and the Kerala Science and Technology Museum were places Aahana had been excited to visit. Surya explored them, feeling her curiosity and love for knowledge guiding him.

As Surya travelled through Kerala, he felt Aahana's presence with him at every step. Each place he visited was a reminder of her dreams and their shared plans. The journey was a process of healing for Surya, helping him come to terms with his loss and find a new sense of purpose. Aahana's spirit lived on in the memories they had created, and Surya vowed to keep her alive in his heart forever.

On the last day of his journey, he felt a deep sense of peace. He remembered a conversation with Aahana about her mother.

Aahana had smiled sadly. "Surya, after my father passed away, my mother and I were all we had. When I got diagnosed, she left everything to come here with me. She promised to go back to our hometown after everything. Please, if you can, visit her for my sake."

"Aahana," Surya had said, "you're not dying anytime soon. Stop thinking about all this."

Present, Surya felt a renewed sense of purpose. He decided to visit Ahana's mother. He didn't know her well, but he felt a strong need to meet her. Returning to Hyderabad, he went straight to his office and asked HR for Ahana's mother's address. The HR was reluctant, but Surya called Phani for help. Phani managed to get the address from a friend of Ahana's.

Early the next morning, Surya arrived at Ahana's hometown. The auto driver took him straight to the house, which was a large, old architectural marvel that exuded a sense of royalty. Surya was awestruck by the house and sat on the steps, waiting for someone to notice him. The house stood tall, its grandeur evident in the intricate carvings and sprawling gardens. The scent of blooming jasmine filled the air, a stark contrast to the heaviness in Surya's heart.

After a while, he heard a voice behind him. "You must be Surya," said a woman.

Surya turned around to see Ahana's mother, a graceful woman with eyes that held the same warmth and depth as Ahana's. "Yes, I am," he replied, his voice tinged with uncertainty.

Ahana's mother sighed, a mixture of sadness and acceptance in her eyes. "So, you finally decided to come. Come on in."

Surya, with a regretful expression, stands in front of Aahana's mother, feeling the weight of not attending the last rites. She gestures for him to come in.

"Aahana's mother: Okay, come on in."

Surya followed her inside, the interior of the house echoing with memories and a sense of history.

"Aahana's mother: Would you like some coffee?"

"Surya: No, I am okay, Aunty."

Despite his refusal, Aahana's mother calls for one of the maids to make coffee. She then turns her attention back to Surya, her eyes reflecting both sadness and understanding.

"Aahana's mother: So, Surya, what are you up to? It took you so long to come."

Surya struggles to find the right words, his mind blank. Aahana's mother continues, her voice gentle but firm.

"Aahana's mother: Aahana already knew that you would not attend her funeral."

Surya looks at her with a puzzled expression, trying to process her words.

"Aahana's mother: Oh, it might be shocking to you, but after her diagnosis, Aahana started writing a diary. She always said it was something to remember her by, something to cherish in her absence. I took my time to open the diary, but when I did, I got to know my daughter even better. She kind of guessed everything that would happen after her passing, and she wrote that you would not be at her funeral but would come to meet me later. She knew you better than you know yourself, Surya."

The guilt of not being there for Aahana's last moments feels even heavier. Trying to shift the focus, he asks softly.

"Surya: How are you coping, Aunty?"

"Aahana's mother: I have been crying since the first time she was diagnosed, so there wasn't much left for me to cry on the day she passed. I feel saddened by her absence, but she prepared me for it. She wrote about what I should do and what I shouldn't. Her words guide me even now."

Aahana's mother pauses, her eyes distant but her voice steady.

"Aahana's mother: Surya, let me be straight and say what she always said: 'A person does not die when they are stabbed by a knife or hit by a bullet or in an accident or cremated. A person really dies when they are forgotten.' Now, tell me, Surya, did Aahana really die that day? I think not, because there is me, and there is you, Surya, who will never let Aahana be forgotten. This is the reality you need to accept."

Surya nods, feeling a mix of grief and determination. He realizes that Aahana's mother is right. He needs to remember Aahana in both her good and bad moments. With curiosity, he looks up and asks.

"Surya: Can I see the diary?"

"Aahana's mother: No."

"Surya: I will only look at the parts where she wrote about me and her, nothing else."

"Aahana's mother: No, Surya. That diary is for me to read."

Surya feels a pang of disappointment. He had hoped to find some solace and resolve through Aahana's words. He sits there, feeling the weight of his sadness.

In the midst of this, the maid brings the coffee and sets it on the table.

"Aahana's mother: Take the coffee."

"Surya: I'm good, Aunty."

"Aahana's mother: Surya, I can't give you the diary, but Aahana left something for you."

Surya's eyes light up with excitement, a spark of hope replacing his earlier despair.

"Surya: What is it that Aahana left for me?"

"Aahana's mother: She left a letter for you."

"Surya: Can I please get it?"

"Aahana's mother: It belongs to you from the start. Let me get it."

Surya waits at the table, the hot coffee untouched. Aahana's mother disappears into another room and returns after a couple of minutes, holding a letter. She hands it to Surya, who takes it with trembling hands.

Surya sits there, feeling the weight of the letter in his hands, knowing it represents his last conversation with Aahana. The familiar scent of Aahana lingers on the paper, and he can almost feel her presence beside him. With a deep breath, he opened the letter, ready to hear Ahana's voice one last time.

A Letter from Aahana to Surya

Hi Surya,

If you are reading this, it means you finally found the courage to face your feelings. I know you well, Surya. You shut down when you're hurt, and that's okay. But I want you to know that it's okay to feel. It's okay to grieve. It's okay to miss me.

And I want you to know that I am still with you in spirit, just as you are always with me. I believe that you are the same Surya, strong and resilient, even in my absence. Please don't let my absence drag you into a loop of sorrow. You don't have to forget me, Surya. I'll always be with you, in your heart. But you need to live your life. Find happiness, find love, find purpose. That's what I want from you.

I want you to remember the good times we shared. Our trips, our conversations, our silly fights. Remember the way we laughed and cried together. Those moments are what make life beautiful.

The last few days we spent together were incredibly happy ones, and that was all because of you. If you hadn't looked at that ID card, or opened that file, or spoken to me, my last days would not have been so meaningful. From the moment I knew about my situation, I had one

wish: to leave this world without any regrets. And you are
the one who made that wish come true.

If you ever have to tell anyone about me, please don't just
count the number of days. Because those days were my
entire life, filled with meaning and joy because of you. To
tell the truth, as I mentioned to you on the train, after my
diagnosis, I didn't go on any trips. The first and only time
was with you, and it was filled with wonderful memories.

I don't expect you to cry for me, but just this once, let
yourself grieve. And then, move on, Surya. Life is all
about moving forward, and that's what you need to do
now. Cry as much as you need, and then, let go.

You made my life complete in those final days.

Take care of my mother in my stead. She needs someone
to be there for her. Visit her often, and let her know that
she's not alone.

And remember, Surya, a person truly dies only when they
are forgotten. Don't let me die. And I know you would
never.

Finally, Like I said before. That I aimed to leave this world
without any regrets,

But you happened, Surya.

With all my love,
Aahana

While Surya in the midst of reading the letter Aahana's mother stood from her chair and open's the window to invite the early sunrays into the house. Those sunrays reaches Surya.

Just like that, Tears streamed down Surya's face as he read the letter. He felt a sense of closure. He looked at Aahana's mother, who was watching him with a gentle smile standing near the window.

Surya cries his soul out; Aahana's mother just approached Surya and gives Surya a gentle hug of console.

"Thank you, Aunty," he said, his voice choked with emotion.

She nodded. "Aahana wanted you to have that. She believed in you, Surya. And so do I."

Surya felt a weight lift off his shoulders. He knew he had a long way to go, but for the first time since Aahana's death, he felt a glimmer of hope. He would carry her memory with him, and he would live his life in a way that honoured her.

As he sat there, sipping the coffee he had initially refused, Surya realized that this was the beginning of a new chapter in his life. A chapter where he would learn to embrace his emotions, find his purpose, and cherish the memories of Aahana, keeping her alive in his heart forever.

A Journey Of Self-discovery

After that story, we resume in the quiet airport lounge where Surya is enjoying his coffee. Surya looks at the readers with a warm smile.

"This is my story," he begins. After a moment's pause, Surya lifts his coffee cup, pointing towards the readers. "I wasn't a coffee person before, but after Ahana came into my life, coffee became my routine. Not only coffee, but so many things changed after Ahana. I began to see the world in a new perspective, which led to a slight change in me over time. Things got better inside me, and I started accepting my emotions as they were. This made my life more comfortable."

He takes a deep breath, his eyes reflecting a mix of sorrow and serenity. "It's been five years since Ahana passed away. I remember the day Ahana's mother handed me the letter Ahana had left for me as if it happened yesterday. That was the day I cried my soul out and wept like never before. After that day, I often visited Ahana's mother, but I never asked about the diary again."

Surya pauses, his gaze distant as he recalls the moment. "One day, out of nowhere, when I visited Ahana's mother, she gave me a piece of paper from Ahana's diary without a single word. The paper seemed freshly torn from the diary, and I could tell just by looking at it. When I held the paper in my hands, it felt like I was holding the entire diary itself."

He carefully unfolds the memory, reciting the words written by Ahana:

These are the places for my next trips with Surya:

- Annavaram, Vizag
- Kerala
- ******
- ******
- ******
- ******
- ******
- ******

"I don't know how many I can complete, but I'm hoping for the best."

Surya's voice softens as he continues, "After seeing that letter, I felt a sense of purpose to fulfil these trips, not just for Ahana, but for my own self-satisfaction."

He takes a final sip of his coffee, a determined glint in his eyes. "So here I am, on a quest to find my self-satisfaction. And Ahana will always live on in my journey."

With that, Surya finishes his coffee and stands up, ready to embark on the next chapter of his life. His story, filled with love, loss, and self-discovery, serves as a poignant reminder that even in the face of heartache, one can find a way to move forward and find peace.

The End.